Sparrow t

GW01326476

A fable fc

Lily F. Wesselhoeft

Alpha Editions

This edition published in 2024

ISBN : 9789361470264

Design and Setting By
Alpha Editions
www.alphaedis.com
Email - info@alphaedis.com

Contents

CHAPTER I.

"LET that sugar-bowl alone, Posy," said Tom, as Posy extracted a lump while they were waiting for Papa and Mamma to come down to breakfast.

"I'm not taking it for *myself*," answered Posy, as plainly as the large lump in her mouth permitted her to speak; "I'm only just getting a lump for Dicky."

"That's a story," said Tom.

"I was only just tasting it to see if it was a real sweet lump," said Posy very distinctly now, for the lump had disappeared. "I didn't mean to eat it, but it went all to pieces in my mouth."

"You might have known it would," said Tom.

"I guess I'd better pick out a real hard lump next time," said Posy; and she made up her mind not to put that one in her mouth, so she only lapped it a little as she walked towards the canary's cage.

Just then a noise was heard from the china-closet, and Tom at once went to see what it was.

"Why, there's a mouse-hole right in the corner of that upper shelf," he said; "I thought it sounded like a mouse gnawing."

"Rats! rats!" called the parrot, whose cage hung in the window by the side of the canary's.

"You're mistaken, ma'am," said Tom; "the barn-cat doesn't give the rats a chance to come into the house,—they live in the barn."

"Rats!" again cried the parrot.

Posy went up to the parrot's cage and looked in.

"How do you do? How's your mother?" asked the parrot, with her head on one side.

"Pretty well, I thank you, Mrs. Polly," answered Posy; and she couldn't resist the temptation of trying to seize the red feathers in Mrs. Polly's tail and give them a little tweak. Mrs. Polly always resented such liberties, and made sudden dives at the chubby fingers; but Posy had learned to be careful, and drew them out in time.

"You wouldn't really bite Posy, would you?" asked the canary.

"No," said Mrs. Polly, "I wouldn't; but I guess you wouldn't like to have your tail pulled every time she gets a chance. It doesn't hurt, you know, but it's very disagreeable. She steals the peanuts out of my cage, too, and eats them. She's a very mischievous child."

"But she's kind and good," answered the canary.

Although this conversation took place between the birds, to the children it seemed as if the canary sang his usual song and Polly chattered in her accustomed way.

Just then Mr. and Mrs. Winton appeared, and the family took their places at the breakfast-table.

Soon a slight rattling was heard among the dishes in the china-closet, and Mr. Winton cautiously approached the closet door and suddenly opened it. A large rat whisked into the hole Tom had discovered.

"We never had a rat in the house before," said Mr. Winton, as he returned to his seat; "I am afraid the house-cat doesn't do her duty. I never thought her so good a ratter as the barn-cat."

"Michael must stop up the hole at once with broken glass and mortar," said Mrs. Winton; "I can't have rats in the house."

"Posy, run into the kitchen and see if Hannah has any more muffins," said Papa; for Katie, who had been both waitress and nurse to Posy, had been gone a few days, and her place had not been supplied.

"How long that child stays!" said Papa, when some minutes had elapsed and she did not return.

"Hannah is rather slow," answered Mamma, "and perhaps the muffins were not quite ready."

A few minutes more passed, but no Posy appeared.

"What can that thumping be?" said Mamma. "I can't imagine what Hannah can be doing. I have heard it for some time. Do run and see what it means, Tom."

"I shouldn't wonder if Posy were up to some mischief," said Tom, as he disappeared.

"What in the world can that boy be doing?" exclaimed Papa, after they had waited some time and neither of the children appeared.

"I will see what the trouble is," said Mamma; but before she rose from her seat Tom reappeared, laughing, and leading Posy, who appeared somewhat confused as she resumed her seat in silence.

"What do you suppose Posy has been doing?" said Tom. "She found Hannah down cellar getting coal, and she locked her down; and then she took the house-kittens and dipped their heads in the pitcher of milk on the table and made 'em drink, and then she brought in the barn-kittens and made them drink too. Hannah said Posy made believe she didn't hear when Hannah pounded on the door and told Posy to let her out. She said she heard Posy running backward and forward, hurrying to get through before anybody came."

"Well," said Posy, "kittens have to be teached to drink milk, you know."

Papa laughed, as he was very apt to do when he heard of Posy's mischief; but when Mamma shook her head at him he stopped and tried to look very serious.

"It was very naughty of you to lock Hannah down cellar, Posy," he said; "you see I can't have any more muffins, for it's time for me to go for the train."

Posy looked very sad to think she had been the cause of so much trouble, and Papa could never bear to see his little girl unhappy; so he caught her in his arms and kissed her, saying,—

"But I can't help loving you, if you *are* naughty."

"Hannah," said Posy, as Hannah entered to take away the breakfast, "my papa says it was very naughty in me to lock you down cellar, but that he loves me still."

"Michael," said Mr. Winton, as the horse was brought around to the door to take him to the depot, "the rats gnawed a hole through the wall in the china-closet last night, and I want you to stop it up with mortar and broken glass."

"All right, sir," answered Michael. "If the barn-cat could be in two places to onst, it's no rats ye'd have in the house. She's a rale knowing baste, is the barn-cat. If you could only see the sinsible way she has wid them kittens of hers. She kapes thim out of doors in foine weather; and when the jew begins to fall, if it's shut the door is, she kapes thim walking about, for fear it's a cold they'll get."

"Let's go and see them," said Tom; and off ran the children as Mr. Winton stepped into the carriage and drove off.

Then, when all was still in the dining-room, a slight noise might have been heard in the china-closet, and a long nose and a pair of very sharp black eyes appeared in the now rat-hole.

Looking cautiously around, and stopping every minute to listen, the rat ventured out. He was quite gray about the mouth from age, and had a particularly vicious look in his shrewd old eyes. Finding all still, he ventured out a little farther, and still farther, and at last slid down from the shelf and entered the dining-room.

Mrs. Polly's quick ears had heard him, and she watched him as he noiselessly moved about, picking up the crumbs that had fallen from the table.

"Hallo!" called out Mrs. Polly.

"Speak a little louder while you're about it," snarled the old rat, who had started at the sound of her voice and listened anxiously to hear if there were danger of detection; and as he spoke he gave a very vicious grin that displayed his long yellow teeth, with one of the front ones broken.

"I haven't time to sit for my portrait this morning," resumed the old rat, as Mrs. Polly continued to gaze steadfastly at him. "You'll know me the next time you see me, I hope!"

"I know you already," said Mrs. Polly; "you're Graywhisker."

"Whew!" exclaimed the old rat, with another grin that showed the broken front tooth; "there's nothing like being famous."

"I've heard of you from my friend the barn-cat," said Mrs. Polly. "She has known you a long time, she says, but you don't care to become very intimate with her;" and Mrs. Polly gave a short laugh that was very irritating to Graywhisker's nerves.

"The old fiend!" he exclaimed angrily; "of all the meddlesome old—"

"Don't get excited," said Mrs. Polly calmly.

"You'd better mind your own business," answered the old rat, "or you'll find yourself in trouble. The barn-cat and you are two very different individuals, and I shan't stand on ceremony with you, I can assure you."

"Do stand on ceremony with me," said Mrs. Polly, with another laugh.

Graywhisker brought his teeth savagely together; but Mrs. Polly kept her cold gray eye on him in such a very unconcerned manner that he evidently thought better of his intention and resumed his search for food.

"Mean people these," he muttered; "not a scrap left. Come, don't be stingy, Mrs. Polly; give me one of your peanuts there. I don't know when I've tasted a peanut,—not since the day Posy left a few and went into the house for a glass of water. She didn't find many left when she came back, though."

"Come and get one if you want it," said Mrs. Polly, eying five freshly roasted peanuts that lay on the bottom of her cage.

Graywhisker watched her shrewdly for an instant, but couldn't determine from her expressionless countenance whether she really meant what she said.

"It's easy enough to pick one out," he said to himself as he began to climb the drapery that hung by the parrot's cage.

Mrs. Polly watched him as he nimbly pulled himself up, and sat with her head inclined slightly forward, following every motion of his. When opposite the cage, he seized it with one of his forepaws, and with the other tried to fish out a particularly fat peanut; but before he could draw it out Mrs. Polly's sharp beak pounced down on the paw, and he gave a squeal of pain.

"Did it taste as well as those you stole from Posy?" asked Mrs. Polly.

"You old vixen!" began Graywhisker, "you—"

"Don't swear," said Mrs. Polly coolly.

The canary had been a silent spectator all this time, and hardly dared to breathe; but when Mrs. Polly pounced on the old rat's paw she gave a nervous flutter.

"Oh! I hadn't noticed you before, my friend," exclaimed Graywhisker, with his horrible grin; "you're a very tender morsel, and I'm not a bit afraid of your soft little beak;" and the old villain began to descend the curtain on Mrs. Polly's side and ascend the one that hung by the canary's cage.

Poor Dicky was completely paralyzed with terror. Up came the gray nose and wicked-looking eyes nearer and nearer, and yet poor Dicky sat without stirring, his terrified eyes fastened on the horrible monster that could crush him with one grasp of his paw. At last he was opposite the cage, and was about to reach out his paw to seize it, when the spell that kept Dicky silent seemed broken, and he fluttered about, uttering cries of terror. The strong paw still held the cage, and the other paw reached in between the wires; but as the frightened bird, in his agitation, fluttered within reach of the relentless paw, Mrs. Polly gave a shrill whistle, and then another louder still.

A rustling was heard in the bushes outside the window, and at the sound Graywhisker descended the curtain and scurried into the closet, disappearing into his hole as the house-cat, with gleaming eyes, jumped on the window-sill and glared around.

"Which way did he go?" she demanded.

The gray nose was pushed cautiously out of the hole, and a voice said,—

"Mrs. House-cat, did you ever get left?"

CHAPTER II.

WHEN Posy caught up the kittens to carry them back to their nest in the barn, it was no wonder that the barn-cat followed her with a distressed and anxious countenance. Posy had been in such a hurry that she had taken one of the barn-kittens and one of the house-kittens!

The barn-cat tried very hard to make the little girl understand her mistake, and ran about her with her tail in the air and crying dismally; but Posy didn't understand, and ran back to the house after putting the kittens in their nest. How the barn-cat did wish she could speak! She looked at the kitten that belonged to the house-cat. It was very pretty,—maltese, with a little white on the breast and about the nose, very like its mother.

"It's rather a good-looking kitten, there's no doubt about that," said the barn-cat, "but to my mind not *half* so pretty and cunning as my little tiger-kitten that Posy left in the kitchen. That house-cat doesn't know how to bring up a family; she'll spoil this one just as she has all of her others. It'll grow up as vain and indolent as she is herself. I'm sure I don't want it here. Come," she said, poking the kitten with her paw, "you just run home again, will you?"

The house-kitten didn't seem to understand what the barn-cat said, for she evidently thought the cat wanted to play with her, and she tried to catch the big paw in both of her little ones.

"Well, you *are* cunning," said the barn-cat. "It's too bad to have you grow up a spoilt child. You'll never be as smart as my kittens, of course, but I've a great mind to keep you and see what you'll make if you are properly brought up."

She didn't like to show the kitten that she was watching her, for it might make her vain; so she pretended to be looking very intently at something out in the yard and gently moved the tip of her tail, but she looked out of the corners of her eyes and saw the little house-kitten at once try to catch it.

"Pretty well," she said to herself, "considering you've never had any instruction. When you're a little older I'll teach you how to crouch and spring, the way I do my own kittens."

Now that the barn-cat had decided to keep the house-kitten, she set about washing it; for Posy had dipped its head so far into the milk-pitcher that it presented a very untidy appearance.

She washed it in a most thorough manner; but the barn-cat was not so gentle in her ways as the house-cat, and the little house-kitten thought her pretty rough.

"You mustn't be a baby and cry for nothing," said the barn-cat, when the kitten gave a mew as the rough tongue lifted her off her feet; "I see you've been coddled too much already."

Just then a plaintive cry was heard from the kitchen, and with one leap the barn-cat was out of her nest and running up to the kitchen door. She didn't dare go in; for there was Hannah, and she knew by experience that she would be driven out if she attempted to enter. What *was* to be done?

The barn-cat jumped on the window-sill and looked in. There was her darling in the box by the stove and crying helplessly for her. The mother cat gave a low mew, which the baby kitten heard and understood just as a human baby understands when its mother speaks soothingly to it.

"Oh dear!" exclaimed the barn-cat, "if I could only get into that kitchen! I know what I'll do. I'll tell Mrs. Polly about it, and see what she advises; she's very wise."

So the barn-cat jumped down from the kitchen window and on the sill of the dining-room window, which stood open. Posy was in the room, and so was Mrs. Winton; but they couldn't understand the language animals converse in.

"Why, there is the barn-cat," cried Posy, "right on the window-seat!"

"Don't frighten her away, but watch her quietly," said Mamma; "I like to have her come about the house;" and Posy was very careful not to make any noise.

"I do believe that barn-cat is telling Polly something, Mamma," said Posy in a low tone; "her keeps mewing, and Polly looks just as if her was listening."

"Polly is certainly very talkative this morning," answered Mamma; "it really does seem as if they were talking together."

"I wish I knew what they were saying," said Posy.

This is what they said:—

"I'm in trouble, Mrs. Polly," began the barn-cat, "and I want you to help me out of it."

"Well," answered Polly, with her very wisest expression, "what's the matter?"

Then the barn-cat told about Posy's mistake, and how anxious it made her to have her kitten away from her.

"It's just like Posy," answered Polly; "she's a very mischievous child. She always tweaks my tail whenever she gets a chance."

"But she's a dear, loving child," said the barn-cat warmly. "How she did cry when they gave away my last kittens!"

"Yes, she's a good little thing," said Polly. "If 'twas anybody else that pulled my tail, I'd give 'em such a nip that they wouldn't try it again in a hurry; but nobody could hurt Posy. She does fish some of my peanuts out of my cage and eat 'em up sometimes, but then she doesn't mean any harm."

"What I want to know is whether you can think of any way for me to get my kitten back," said the barn-cat. "I tried to make Posy understand what a dreadful mistake she'd made, but she was in such a hurry she didn't see it."

Mrs. Polly put her head on one side in a very knowing and contemplative manner. After a few moments' reflection she said, "The thing to do is to get Hannah out of the kitchen for a while."

"That's very evident," said the canary, who had been listening attentively and didn't like to be left out of the conversation.

"If it's so very evident," said Mrs. Polly, bristling up, "why don't you do it?"

"I didn't say *I* could do it; but if I could talk as you can, I would," answered the canary good-naturedly.

"How would you do it, pray?" asked Mrs. Polly in an irritable tone.

"Why, I'd call Hannah the way Mrs. Winton does. I heard you call her the other day, and I declare I wouldn't have believed it wasn't she. I never knew a bird that could talk as plainly as you do."

The canary was so good-natured that Mrs. Polly was rather ashamed of her ill-temper, and gave a sneeze and cough to hide her embarrassment.

"Well," she said, after a pause, "perhaps that's as good a way as any other. I *did* think of yelling to make her think I'd got my head caught between the wires, but Posy doesn't like to hear such a noise. You go 'round to the kitchen door," she said to the barn-cat; "and when Hannah leaves the kitchen you just dart in, seize your kitten, and run off with it."

The barn-cat hardly waited to hear the last words, and ran around to the kitchen door. She had hardly arrived there when she heard Polly call

"Hannah!" so exactly like Mrs. Winton that Hannah dropped the broom with which she was sweeping the floor, and answering, "Yes, ma'am," hurried into the dining-room.

In darted the barn-cat, caught up her darling in her mouth, and had it back in her own nest in the barn before Hannah had discovered how Polly had "fooled" her, as she called it.

But when the house-cat came home from her visit, imagine what was her surprise and grief to find one of her babies gone!

"That barn-cat!" she exclaimed, "I believe she has stolen it because it's so much prettier than her common-looking babies. She was always as jealous as she could be of them!" and out to the barn went the house-cat.

"I never visited her before," she said to herself, "she's so countrified in her ways and lives in a barn; but I must see if she's got my baby."

The barn-cat knew what she was coming for as soon as she caught sight of her.

"I want my kitten," said the house-cat, going up to the box; and she stepped very daintily and held her head very high, as if she were afraid of soiling her shining fur. "I should think you'd be ashamed of yourself to slink into the house and steal my kitten! But I don't suppose you know any better, as you've never been used to good society."

"I didn't steal your kitten! I don't want your old kitten; it isn't half so smart or pretty as mine are."

"Indeed!" answered the house-cat with a toss of her head. "Your common-looking tiger-kittens! Look at my baby's soft skin and her gentle little ways!"

"I'll leave it to Posy if mine are not the smartest and handsomest," answered the barn-cat angrily. "They had hard work to get anybody to take your kittens the last time, and mine were spoken for before they had their eyes open!"

The house-cat was very angry, but she knew there was truth in what the barn-cat said; so she only repeated, "Indeed!" in a very scornful manner, and tossed her head.

"You coddle your children too much," continued the barn-cat. "You keep them by the warm stove, and don't take them out doors often enough. That makes them tender."

"When I want your advice I'll ask for it," answered the house-cat loftily, as she took up her kitten and went home with it.

"It was a pretty enough kitten, though I wasn't going to tell her so," said the barn-cat to herself. "I think I could have made a smart kitten of it, but it will only be spoiled now;" and the barn-cat sighed as she lapped a rough spot on one of her kitten's ears.

"Meaw! meaw!" was heard in plaintive tones just outside the barn-door. It was a new voice, and the barn-cat quickly sprang up to see what was the matter. On the step of the barn-door sat a little gray kitten with a rough and muddy fur, who looked as if she had travelled a long way. She kept uttering sad little mews; and as she turned her head towards the barn-cat the latter saw that she was blind.

The Blind Kitten

CHAPTER III.

"WELL, where did you come from, I should like to know?" asked the barn-cat sharply; for the little gray kitten didn't present a very respectable appearance, and she was very particular about the company her family kept.

"Oh! I've come a long, long way," said the gray kitten in a sad little voice, "all the way from the other side of the town, and I am very tired."

"Why didn't you stay at home?" said the barn-cat. "Home's the best place for young people."

"I haven't got any home," sighed the gray kitten.

"That's a likely story," said the barn-cat shortly. "Where's your mother? She must be a nice kind of a mother not to provide a home for her children. Every cat can do that."

"I haven't got any mother," said the little gray kitten sadly.

The barn-cat gave her nose a sharp rub with her paw,—a habit she had when her feelings were touched.

"Well, you live somewhere, I suppose. Who gives you food? You can't live on air."

"Last night I slept in a hollow tree," said the gray kitten, "and I assure you I don't get much to eat. If it hadn't been for a little girl sharing her food with me, I should have starved long ago, for I am 'most blind and can't see well enough to make my own living."

"I should like to hear your story," said the barn-cat, "and then we'll see what can be done for you. Let me see—" and she rubbed her ear in a contemplative way. "I think we'd better let Mrs. Polly and the canary hear your story, too. They are both pretty wise, and three heads are better than one any day. There comes that house-cat; she's nobody."

So the barn-cat led the way to the open window where the parrot's and canary's cages were hanging.

"What under the sun have you got there?" asked Mrs. Polly, eying the poor little gray kitten shrewdly.

The barn-cat had jumped on the window-seat, but the gray kitten had modestly seated herself on the ground under the window. The house-cat, too, had joined the group, and placed herself where she could watch the little gray kitten. She stared at the poor little thing so scornfully that she didn't know which way to look; so she looked on the ground and presented a very miserable appearance indeed, with her soiled and rumpled fur and her poor half-blind eyes.

"Where did you pick her up?" asked Mrs. Polly.

"I don't know much more about her than you do," answered the barn-cat. "I found her a few minutes ago on the door-step of the barn, and she tells me she has come from the other side of the town, and that she hasn't any mother. I thought you'd better see her and hear her story, and perhaps you'd think of something that could be done for her."

Mrs. Polly put on her wise look and gave a little Ahem! for it always gratified her to be looked up to and asked for advice.

Meanwhile the house-cat sat staring the poor gray kitten out of countenance. "*My* advice is to send her back where she came from," she said. "Anybody can see that she's only a tramp. I won't have *my* children taught any of her common ways. Besides, there are too many cats around already," she added, eying the barn-cat so scornfully that it was very evident she referred to her and her kittens.

"Whoever she is and wherever she comes from, it's as plain as the nose on your face that she's been well brought up," answered the barn-cat quickly. "She's quiet and lady-like in her manners, and that's more than can be said of some who've had the best of advantages."

"She's a common kitten, probably brought up in a barn," said the house-cat contemptuously, "and has no style whatever."

This was too much for the barn-cat's endurance, and she gave an angry spit, when the canary, who was always the peace-maker, interposed.

"Whatever she may be," said the canary gently, "she's neglected and unfortunate; so, if Mrs. Polly will find out her story, I'm sure she will find a way to help her out of her troubles. If her wise head can't, I don't know whose can."

"Well," said Mrs. Polly, "I should have done so long ago if our friends here hadn't taken up so much time in disputing. Now, little gray kitten, tell us all you know about yourself,—where you were born, and how it happens that you are left alone in this big world to take care of yourself."

"I can't remember very much about myself," began the little gray kitten in a plaintive voice, "but I know we were always poor. My mother worked very hard to support us, for the woman who kept us was very mean and never gave us anything to eat. I have heard my mother say she was the meanest woman she ever knew. She said she had heard her say that she

- 13 -

kept a cat to get rid of the rats and mice, and that she expected her to earn her own living."

"Well," interrupted the barn-cat, "that is all very well for a single cat; but when a cat has a young family it comes pretty hard to keep them supplied with food. I never let my children eat mice; it doesn't agree with them,—gives 'em the stomach-ache and makes 'em fitty."

"It's no harm to give 'em a mouse to play with," said the house-cat; "I often do mine."

"When you catch one, which isn't often," said the barn-cat in an undertone.

"What was that you said?" asked the house-cat sharply; "be kind enough to say it a little louder."

"Oh, come, come," put in the canary, "do let the gray kitten go on with her story. You were telling us that your mother had to catch all the food for you."

"Yes," continued the little gray kitten, "so she did. She often brought us mice, and sometimes a bird,—birds agreed best with us, she said."

"Dear me!" exclaimed the canary with a shudder, "what a very bloodthirsty cat your mother must have been!"

"Excuse me, I didn't mean to hurt your feelings," said the little gray kitten, so politely that Mrs. Polly said to herself with a little nod of satisfaction,—

"Very well brought up, indeed!"

"Go on, my dear, with your story," said Mrs. Polly, aloud. "How many were there of you?"

"There were only my brother and myself," answered the little gray kitten. "My mother said there were two others, but they died very young,— before they had their eyes open. She said she thought they didn't have enough to eat."

"Well, how about your mother? I'm anxious to hear about her," said the barn-cat.

"It makes me very sad to think about it," continued the little gray kitten, almost crying. "One day my mother told me and my brother that she was going to teach us how to hunt. It was the first time we had been out of doors; we lived in an old shed. It was a very pleasant day, and the air was so fresh, and the birds did look so tempting— I beg your pardon," she added, as the canary began to flutter nervously.

"Never mind; go on with your story," said the canary good-naturedly. "It's your nature; you aren't to blame."

The little gray kitten was so embarrassed by this interruption that she forgot where she had left off in her story; but then she was so very little!

"You were saying," said Mrs. Polly, "that your mother took you out of doors to teach you to hunt."

"Oh yes," answered the gray kitten, "so I was. Well, it was very pleasant, and we enjoyed ourselves very much, and I caught a little field-mouse, and so did my brother; and our mother praised us, and said that after all perhaps we would turn out smarter cats than if we had been brought up to have everything we wanted, for then we might have become lazy."

"Very true, indeed," interrupted the barn-cat, with a triumphant glance at the house-cat. "Your mother must have been a very sensible cat!"

"Well, then what happened, little one?" asked Mrs. Polly; for the gray kitten was again thrown off her balance by the interruption.

"The next is very sad, indeed," said the gray kitten. "We were going home, so happy to think our dear mother was so pleased with us, when all at once we heard a dreadful noise. My brother and I were frightened half to death, for we had never heard a noise like it. My mother said it was a dog, and there was a boy with it,—a bad boy; my mother said all boys were bad—"

"Not *all* boys," said the barn-cat. "Tom isn't a bad boy; he wouldn't hurt a kitten for the world. I'd trust him anywhere with my kittens."

"He isn't so mischievous as Posy is," said the house-cat.

"Posy isn't mischievous," said the barn-cat warmly; "she doesn't mean to do mischief. You can't call it mischief when she thinks she's doing something to help you all the time."

"Please don't interrupt so often," said the canary; "you said, little kitten, that a big dog and a boy came up."

"Yes," continued the little gray kitten; "and as soon as the boy saw us he said, 'Hie, Rover, seize 'em, sir!' and the big dog, looking, oh, so fierce and angry, rushed at us with his mouth wide open, and making that dreadful noise. There was a tree near us, and my mother told my brother and me to climb up the tree as quickly as we could. My poor mother gave us the first chance, for she knew we couldn't climb as well as she could, and she stood at the foot of the tree with her fur all bristling up and spitting at the big dog. We got up to the first branches where the dog couldn't reach us; but before my poor mother had time to follow us the big dog seized her, and gave her one shake and killed her."

Her hearers were very quiet as the little gray kitten ceased and sat crying softly to herself. The barn-cat gave her nose a sharp rub with her paw, and then jumped down and examined very carefully a hole under the window, as if she expected to find a mouse there. Her feelings were very much touched, for she couldn't help thinking how dreadful it would be if her little kittens were left without a mother to care for them.

"Well," she said, after a pause, coming back to her place on the window-sill, "what did your brother and you do then?"

"We waited till the boy and the big dog were gone," said the little gray kitten, "and then we climbed down from the tree and went home. It was very lonely in the old shed, and we almost starved to death, for we were too small to catch mice enough to satisfy our appetites. My brother got tired of living so, and said he was going to try to find a better home where they would feed him, but I stayed where I was."

"How about that girl you said used to feed you?" asked the house-cat.

"She was a poor little girl who didn't have any mother either, and the woman I belonged to made her work hard and gave her very little to eat; but she pitied me, and often went hungry herself to share her food with me."

"What made your eyes so bad, my dear?" asked Mrs. Polly kindly.

"I think it must have been the cold; it was very cold in the shed."

There was a few minutes' silence, and then Mrs. Polly said,—

"I have been thinking the matter over, and I believe the best thing to do is to get Posy to help us. You put yourself in the way where she'll see you," she said to the little gray kitten, "and all will be well."

The poor little girl and the blind kitten.—*Page* 45.

CHAPTER IV.

POSY and Tom were seated on the kitchen door-step, and the two house-kittens lay in Posy's lap. Posy was in a very thoughtful mood, and sat watching the kittens in silence.

"I've been wondering, Tom," she said at last, "where God keeps his babies that haven't got any wings."

"Why, babies don't ever have wings, Posy," said Tom.

"Yes, they do, the angel babies. I mean the ones he brings down here to people."

"Oh!" said Tom, "I suppose he has some nice place to keep 'em in."

"I should think," said Posy thoughtfully, "that we might see Him when he goes around from house to house."

"Why, of course we can't," answered Tom decidedly.

Posy played with the kittens in her lap.

"Come, Kitty, and have your bonnet on," she said, folding her handkerchief over the head of one of the kittens and tying it under her chin. "Poor thing, you haven't got a single dress after your name, and I must make you one. And I guess I'd better make some little cow-catchers around your forehead; they are very becoming to your little rosy face."

"Cow-catchers!" laughed Tom. "You mean beau-catchers! What a little goosie you are, Posy!"

"I know that just as well as you can," answered Posy, blushing; and she thought it best to turn the conversation.

"Tom," she said, "I guess I shall marry you when I'm grown up,—either you or Papa."

"People can't marry their fathers!" said Tom, with an air of superior wisdom, "because they've got married already, you know."

"Well, then, I shall marry you, because I love you so much. People can marry their brothers, can't they, Tom?"

"I don't know about that," answered Tom shrewdly.

"Well, then, let me see—who shall I marry? I *did* think of marrying Mary Weston, but her's married already, you know. I guess I'll marry Mr. Dawson."

"I know why," said Tom quickly; "it's because he's got some puppies! Oh, you selfish girl!"

"I don't care," said poor Posy in a very crestfallen manner; "I'd give you one of the puppies, Tom."

"I guess Mr. Dawson will be out of the world long before you're ready to git married, Posy," said Hannah, who had been listening to the conversation between the children; "he must be nigh onto seventy if he's a day. Well, Tom, who do you intend to marry?"

"If I marry for love," answered Tom, "I shall marry Auntie; but if I marry for money, I shall marry Katie Thomas, because her father's got more money than old Mr. Thornton, and he's got a hundred dollars in the bank."

"Well, I never!" said Hannah; "but I guess I'd better be about my work. I wish that lazy Michael would bring me in some wood. He grows worse every day. I bet he's asleep somewhere,—he usually *is* asleep when there's anything to be done."

"He's gone to get Major shod," said Tom; "I saw him go down the yard with him."

"There he comes!" said Posy, as a man appeared leading a handsome chestnut horse up the yard.

"Good-morning, Michael," called Posy when he was opposite the kitchen door.

"Good-morning, Miss," answered Michael.

"Have you had a nap to-day, Michael?" asked Posy in her sweetest way.

"No, Miss," answered Michael, as he led the horse into the barn.

"That child does beat anything I ever see," said Hannah, laughing, as she went about her work again.

Suddenly a dreadful noise was heard from the direction of the dining-room window,—shrieks as if somebody were in great distress.

"Polly's got her head caught between the wires," cried Tom, jumping up and running around to the window. Posy quickly dumped the kittens into their nest and followed him as fast as she could. As soon as they appeared Polly burst into a loud laugh.

"The next time I shan't believe you, ma'am, you've fooled me so many times," said Tom.

"Oh, Tom," cried Posy, "look, see! see this poor little gray kitten! Poor thing, her's awful thin, and her looks as if her didn't have any home."

"Why, she's blind!" said Tom. "Poor kitty, come, I won't hurt you;" and he lifted the little gray kitten very gently, and sat down on the piazza step softly stroking it.

"Her isn't one bit afraid of us," said Posy, seating herself beside Tom and stroking the kitten too. "Her knows we won't hurt her, don't her, Tom?"

The little gray kitten had heard all about the children, and felt perfectly secure with them.

"Her's purring!" cried Posy joyfully. "I mean to ask Mamma if I can keep her." And off ran Posy to Mamma's room.

"There's a poor little gray kitten out doors, Mamma," said Posy, all out of breath from hurrying, "and her's blind of one eye. Can't I keep her and take care of her? Her looks like her didn't have any home at all."

"Yes," said Mamma, "you may ask Hannah to give you a saucer of milk for her."

"Her's blind of *both* eyes," cried Posy, bursting into tears; "but I thought you wouldn't let me keep her if you knew it."

"Why, my dear little girl," answered Mamma, drawing Posy to her side, "I love to have you kind to animals, and particularly so to those that are helpless and can't take care of themselves. Don't cry, my darling, you shall give this poor little kitten a comfortable home, and make her as happy as if she were not blind."

"But it makes me feel bad to think her can't see," said Posy, sobbing.

"Think, my darling, how much more comfortable you can make her than she has ever been before; and perhaps it is not so bad as you think,— she may not be wholly blind."

So Mamma put down her sewing, and went with Posy to look at the little gray kitten, who all this time had been purring away contentedly in Tom's lap.

"Oh no," said Mamma, "she isn't wholly blind, she can see out of one eye; and we will bathe her eyes with some warm water and a soft sponge, and she will feel as comfortable as possible."

"I knew how it would be," said the parrot to the canary, as the kitten was carried off to the kitchen to be fed.

"Kind people, every one of them," answered the canary, hopping about for joy. "Hallo! what's the barn-cat up to? Do look at her!"

The barn-cat was creeping cautiously along the yard, her body almost touching the ground and her eyes glowing with eagerness. Sometimes she stopped for an instant and swished her tail excitedly, then went on again. The canary and Mrs. Polly soon saw what it was that excited her so. A little sparrow sat on a stone a few rods off, pluming his feathers in a very unconcerned manner. The barn-cat stopped and wriggled her body for a final spring, when all at once Mrs. Polly screamed out, "Scat! scat!" in so loud a voice and so exactly like a human being that the barn-cat stopped in her spring and the sparrow flew up into a bush opposite the dining-room window.

Certainly the sparrow was a very rowdy-looking bird. His feathers were rumpled and many of them broken, and he had a very independent air that was a great contrast to the refined manner of the well-kept canary.

"Who are you, pray?" asked Mrs. Polly, eying the new-comer curiously.

"Can't you see?" answered the sparrow in a hoarse voice.

"It's very evident you're a tramp," said Mrs. Polly. "What do you want here?"

"I didn't know you'd got a lease of the place, or I wouldn't have come," answered the sparrow pertly.

"Come now, keep a civil tongue in your head," said Mrs. Polly. "You'll find it to your advantage. Where do you live?"

"Wherever I can. Sometimes in one place, sometimes in another."

"That looks bad," said Mrs. Polly gravely. "Did you ever hear the proverb that 'rolling stones gather no moss'?"

"Now look here, Mrs. Parrot, I haven't asked anything of you, and I ain't going to. I acknowledge I'm a tramp, if having no home makes a bird one. I get my food where I can, but I don't do anybody any harm. If I prefer to live that way, whose business is it but my own?"

"You've been fighting, I see," said Mrs. Polly gravely; "'tisn't respectable."

"Now look here, ma'am! You're kept in a cage, and have your food given you regular, and don't have to trouble yourself about where your next meal is to come from. I live where I can, pick up my own meals where I can find 'em; if I can't find 'em I go without. I sleep out in all kinds of weather, and that makes my feathers rough and my voice hoarse; but I want you to understand that I'm just as good a fellow as if I had a red tail and a hooked nose."

"That's very true," said the good-natured canary, "I should like to make your acquaintance. You go about so much you must see and hear a good many things that we don't."

"Well, I guess I could tell you a thing or two that would make your feathers curl," answered the stranger.

Just then the children came along with the little gray kitten that had been washed and fed, and seated themselves on the steps of the piazza.

"Hallo!" called out the sparrow to the little gray kitten, "how in the world did you turn up here?"

"Do you know her?" asked Mrs. Polly.

"Well, I should rather think I did, seeing as I have lived, as you might say, in the same family."

"How is little Nancy?" asked the little gray kitten. "I have worried a good deal about that child since I left home. That's the little girl I told you was so kind to me," she said in explanation to the parrot.

"She's well," answered the sparrow, "but I pity the poor thing with all my heart. This morning she came out and sat on the door-step, and I saw she was crying, and she says to me, 'Billy' (she always called me Billy), 'I can't give you anything to eat this morning because I haven't got anything myself, and I didn't get any supper last night either, Billy, because I couldn't sell any matches.' She didn't know I sensed what she was saying, but I did. Look here! You seem pretty well off around here. I see the little gray kitten has fallen into good hands. Can't you do something for a poor child that's half starved and abused?"

"Oh, do, Mrs. Polly!" said the little gray kitten. "You were so kind to me, do find some way to get that poor little Nancy with these good people."

"Well," said Mrs. Polly, "I'll think it over and see what can be done about it."

"How loud this gray kitten does purr," said Posy. "I guess her's telling us how happy her is to get here, don't you, Tom?"

"Posy and Tom were seated on the kitchen door-step."—*Page* <u>47.</u>

CHAPTER V.

THE next morning Major, the horse, was eagerly eating his breakfast of nice fresh oats. He was an easy-tempered fellow, but this morning he was greatly annoyed, and with good reason; he was very hungry and must share his breakfast with several rats that were bold enough to venture into his manger and steal his oats from before his very eyes.

"I do wish my friend the barn-cat would not take the opportunity to go out while I am eating," said Major to himself. "I knew how it would be when she told me she must go and see Mrs. Polly about this plan of bringing that child Nancy here. 'When the cat's away the mice will play;' and what's more, the rats too. Here, old Graywhisker, you come any nearer and I'll bite off your tail!"

"I'd like to see you do it," snarled the old rat; and as he spoke he showed his long yellow teeth with one of them broken off, which gave him a very disagreeable expression. "I'd like to see you stop us from eating a few of your oats. You're too fat already; I heard Mr. Winton tell Michael so the other day."

"I should be loath to tell you what I've heard him say about you," answered Major angrily; "you wouldn't sleep very well nights if I did."

The old rat forgot his usual caution, and came nearer to Major's face than ever before; and Major, his patience gone, gave a sudden snort and pushed them all out of the manger with his nose. Then when he was left alone he went on eating his breakfast. After that he found himself becoming very sleepy, and shutting his eyes he fell into a doze. As he slept the old rat stole quietly out of his hole and looked cautiously about.

"Come," he said to the others, "come out on the barn floor, for I have something of importance to say to you, and this is a good time, as Major is asleep, and the barn-cat off. Here, you Silvertail, you keep a sharp lookout in every direction, and tell me if you see the barn-cat coming."

The young rat addressed, quickly climbed on the window-sill, whence he could command a fine view of the entrances to the barn.

"Do you see anything of the barn-cat?" asked the old rat.

"Yes, I see her right in front of the dining-room window; and by the way she swishes her tail I know she's talking pretty fast."

"Well, let her swish," answered the old rat; "she'll find there are some people in the world as smart as she is."

The old rat, Graywhisker, seated himself, and the other rats came flocking out of their holes and placed themselves in a circle about him. Some of them brought their young families, as they couldn't trust them alone.

"I don't see any of our friends the mice," said Graywhisker, looking about with his sharp old eyes. "Some of you young fellows run over to Mrs. Silverskin, and tell her I want to see her at once; and be quick about it too."

Two young rats started off, and began to climb to the hay-mow, playing tag on the way.

"Here, none of your fooling!" called out the old rat sharply, as one of them gave a loud squeak.

This squeak awoke Major from his nap, and hearing voices his curiosity was aroused. "I guess I'll keep my ears open, and perhaps I shall hear something," he said to himself; "you can't trust these rats out of your sight."

So Major made believe asleep, and even gave a snore occasionally to mislead the rats; and he did completely mystify them.

Soon the two young rats returned, scampering headlong down from the mow, and followed more leisurely by Mrs. Silverskin, who had a very timid, gentle air, and who looked very small and refined by the side of the great clumsy rats with their bold countenances.

"Now sit still and listen with all your ears," began old Graywhisker, "for I've something of importance to say, and our time is short, as that arch fiend, the barn-cat, may return at any moment. To cut a long matter short, the barn-cat has introduced another cat here. To be sure, she's half blind, and a half-grown kitten, but still she's to be dreaded. Then there's been a sparrow loafing around here lately, and they're laying a plot this very minute to get a good-for-nothing girl here, but we'll put a stop to that. I hid under the piazza yesterday and heard the whole story,—how this girl had fed the lazy sparrow and the half-blind kitten (it's good enough for her, and I wish she was blind of both eyes), and how they must think of some way to get this poor child among these good people. They're talking it over now, and I've set Sharpears to watch and tell me what they've said. The barn-cat said that if they could arrange matters so that Posy could hear her story, she would bring it all about. Posy, indeed! I hate that child! She makes a dreadful fuss over all the other animals, but I heard her say the other day to the barn-cat, 'You mustn't catch the pretty little birdies, kitty, but you can catch just as many of the great ugly rats as you've a mind to.' I paid her off, though; I stole her piece of cake that she laid down on the door-step when she went into the house, and she felt awfully about it. It was real fun to see how disappointed she was when she came back and found it gone."

Here Mrs. Silverskin, who had sat meekly listening, spoke in a soft little voice,—

"I don't believe Posy could see any animal suffer. I saw her sprinkle some crumbs down in front of a hole one day, and say, 'These are for the little mice to eat.'"

"Oh, yes! you take her part, do you?" said old Graywhisker, fiercely glaring at the poor little mouse. "If that is your opinion, you just clear out of my barn. I want you to understand that I won't have any hypocrites around these premises."

"You can't call me a hypocrite," said the little mouse meekly; "I only said that Posy was a kind-hearted child. I am sure I dislike the barn-cat as much as you do, and it gives me great uneasiness to think there's another of that species on the premises if she is half blind. I am afraid our children will get careless, thinking she can't see them, and some day venture too near. I am sure I shall never have another easy moment;" and Mrs. Silverskin looked more anxious than ever.

"Here comes Sharpears creeping along this way," called out Silvertail from the window.

The whole company looked anxiously in the direction of their private entrance, and Sharpears soon appeared at the opening.

"Well," said old Graywhisker impatiently, "what did you hear?"

"In the first place," began Sharpears, "Major has been complaining that we eat too many of his oats. He says that when the barn-cat's away we bother him so that he can't take any comfort in his eating."

"He eats too much," said Graywhisker; "that's what's the matter with him. Just hear him snore! He'll go off in a fit of apoplexy one of these days! I wish he would!"

"The barn-cat said she did her best; that she knew the rats and mice did take advantage of her absence, but that she was going to train the gray kitten to watch while she was away."

"We'll fix that gray kitten," snarled the old rat, bringing his long yellow teeth together in a very unpleasant manner.

"After that they had a long talk about how they could bring it about to get that child Nancy here that had fed the sparrow and the gray kitten.

Feeding the kitten, indeed! as if there were not cats enough around already! When I came away they were talking about having the sparrow entice her here some way or other."

"Why didn't you stay and hear it out?" said the old rat savagely. "I thought you had more sense."

"Well, all at once that disagreeable Polly (she's always minding everybody's business but her own) said, 'I do believe there's a rat under that piazza.' I didn't wait to hear any more, I can tell you, but slunk off just as the barn-cat jumped down to find out where the noise came from."

"Here comes the barn-cat!" called out Silvertail from the window; and instantly the whole company darted to their holes, as the barn-cat appeared at the head of the stairs.

The barn-cat put her nose up in the air and sniffed. "Those rats and mice have been about, sure as you live!" she said. "I must teach the gray kitten to keep a sharp lookout while I'm away. Hallo!" she called to Major, "how are you getting on?"

"All right," answered Major; "I've important news for you. I made believe asleep just now, and heard a thing or two. The rats know exactly what you're plotting, for they set a spy to listen to your conversation this morning. They know you're going to try to get that girl here, and they're going to stop it if they can, because she fed the little gray kitten."

"I'd like to see 'em do it," said the barn-cat.

"They can annoy you, though, in a great many ways," said Major; "and, to tell the truth, I'm afraid they're going to plot against the gray kitten. They all seemed full of spite against her."

"I'd like to see 'em touch a hair of her head!" exclaimed the barn-cat ferociously.

"Here comes that dear child, Posy, with your breakfast," said Major, as Posy appeared, carrying a plate and followed by Tom with a saucer of milk.

"Here, kitty," called Posy; "I've brought you some nice milk and some critters all cut up fine. Are they *critters* or fritters?" she asked, turning to Tom.

"*Fritters*, of course," answered Tom. "You do manage to get things twisted about, Posy. Papa says you are a real Mrs. Malaprop."

"Kitty," said Posy, putting her hand in her pocket and drawing out a little package, "I have brought you the beautifulest present you ever had in all your life;" and Posy began to undo the paper.

Major and Graywhisker.

CHAPTER VI.

POSY undid the package, and took out a pretty collar of red leather with a little padlock hanging from it.

"Come, kitty, and have on your new collar," said Posy. "They say you're not so handsome as the house-cat, so I must make you look as well as I can, and you're dear if you're not handsome."

The barn-cat stood very still while Posy fitted on the collar and fastened the padlock.

"It's a little bit loose for you," said Posy, "but that is better than to have it too tight, isn't it, Tom?"

"See how proud she feels," said Tom; "she likes to hear the padlock rattle when she moves."

"It is really a very stylish affair," said the barn-cat to herself, "and I must smarten myself up a little. I wonder what the house-cat will say now!"

"It's pretty loose for her," said Tom; "I'm afraid she'll lose it off. Let's take it up another notch."

"No," said Posy decidedly; "Mamma said if it was too tight it would make her uncomf'table."

"Well, if she loses it, don't bawl," answered Tom.

"I shan't bawl," said Posy indignantly.

The children gave a look at the kittens, and then went away; and the barn-cat ate her breakfast contentedly, stopping occasionally to give her head a shake, that she might have the satisfaction of hearing the padlock rattle.

That afternoon the barn-cat called the little gray kitten to her, and told her she wanted her to keep watch while she went to fulfil a very important engagement with Mrs. Polly and the canary.

"Take good care of the kittens, and don't let the rats annoy Major while he is eating. He complains a good deal of them lately."

The little gray kitten promised to do all she was told; and off hurried the barn-cat, having carefully washed herself and smoothed her fur as neatly as she could.

While she was making these preparations, she did not see a pair of sharp little black eyes watching all her movements from a beam above.

"I know what all this means," said the owner of the sharp black eyes, "but you have to get up pretty early to get the start of an old rat;" and he smiled a very vicious smile that displayed his long yellow teeth with one of them broken off.

"I guess I'd better go myself," continued old Graywhisker; "these young fellows are too giddy to be trusted, and after all we mustn't expect to find old heads on young shoulders;" and he stroked his gray beard with a very satisfied air.

After the barn-cat had gone, he followed cautiously at a distance. He knew better than to trust himself under the piazza again; so he wedged himself into a space between the house and a large stone, just around the corner, where he could hear without being detected. When he was comfortably settled, he smiled again to himself to think how wise he was.

"Well," he heard Polly say, "here we are again, except the sparrow,—he's late."

"Just as likely as not we'll never see him again," said the barn-cat. "You can't place any reliance on these tramps. I never did like his looks, I must confess."

"I don't believe he's a bad fellow at heart," said the canary; "he seemed very anxious to have that little girl taken care of, and very grateful for what she did for him. Bad people are not grateful, you know."

"I wish he would settle down and become steady," said Mrs. Polly, "but I'm afraid there's no hope of that. Yesterday a friend of his flying by stopped and had a few minutes' chat with me. He says the sparrow has a wife and several children, but that he's away half the time, and neglects his family dreadfully, though he's good enough to them when he's at home. It's just as I suspected,—he's lazy and shiftless."

"Well, I confess, that's just what I thought of him," said the barn-cat. "I never did fancy his looks from the first; but he's useful to us, and we must put up with his failings."

A slight rustling in a neighboring bush made them all look in that direction; and there sat the subject of their conversation, and judging from the roguish twinkle in his eyes, he had evidently heard the whole conversation.

"Sorry to have kept you waiting," he said good-naturedly, "but was detained on very important business. Hope I see you as well as usual, ma'am, and that you haven't missed me too much," he said to the barn-cat with a sly wink.

The barn-cat thought it more dignified not to answer this familiar speech, and looked straight before her.

"Well," said Mrs. Polly, "let's make the most of our time now that we are all together."

"First of all," said the barn-cat, "I want to tell you that yesterday we were watched. Old Graywhisker had set a spy to listen to our conversation, and he reported every word that was said. However, I'd like to see him prevent us from carrying out our plans. I'll just give a look under the piazza before we begin; that's where he was yesterday, and the only place where he could hide."

Graywhisker kept very still while the barn-cat investigated the piazza, and hardly dared breathe; but when she returned to her place again, saying, "There's nobody there now, you may be sure of that," he smiled again, and placing his right paw against his nose waggled it in a very exultant manner.

"Now," said Mrs. Polly, "what we have to do is to decide how we can get the child Nancy here. I have a plan of my own that I will mention, and I'd like to have you express your opinions freely."

Meanwhile the sparrow, who was seated on a slender branch opposite the window, was amusing himself by standing first on one leg and then on the other and having a fine see-saw all by himself. The barn-cat watched him eagerly; and his motions were so graceful, and he was so plump, that she quite forgot where she was, and sat swishing her tail in a very tiger-like manner, and was about to give a spring when Mrs. Polly's keen eyes caught sight of her, and she called out,—

"Hallo there! what are you about?"

The barn-cat was really ashamed to have so forgotten herself, and was greatly embarrassed.

"What can you expect of a cat that's been brought up in a barn?" said the house-cat scornfully. "That comes of letting such common people associate with those who have been accustomed to good society!"

The barn-cat was not ready as usual with an answer to this taunt from her enemy, for she knew she had been guilty of very great rudeness; and Mrs. Polly, knowing that although her manners were rough her heart was a very good one, kindly went on with her remarks:—

"The plan I have thought of is this: You have all of you seen how often Posy sits on the piazza and cuts dolls' dresses out of bright-colored pieces of ribbon and silk. Now there is nothing in the world, I have noticed, that pleases a little girl so much as those bright colors, and we will take advantage of that. The next time Posy brings out her ribbons we must get her out of the way long enough for one of you to steal the prettiest one, and then the sparrow can use it to entice the child Nancy with."

"But who is to steal the ribbon?" asked the house-cat.

"I should say the sparrow was the one to do that," answered Mrs. Polly; "he can fly down and pick one out and fly off with it."

"Very good," said the sparrow; "but how are you going to make Posy leave her ribbons long enough?"

"I've called 'em so many times lately," said Mrs. Polly, "that they begin to suspect me; and Tom said the other day that I had fooled him so many times that he shouldn't come again if I called. Let me see—" and Mrs. Polly put on her very wisest expression.

"There's one way we could fix it," said the sparrow. "Here's my friend the barn-cat; she's so fond of me she can't have me near enough. Suppose I place myself where Posy can see me, and the barn-cat can make believe spring at me just as she did a few minutes ago. The dear thing! we know she does it out of affection for me, but Posy will think she's in earnest."

"A very good plan," said Mrs. Polly. "Really quite a bright idea," she said in an undertone to the canary, "though it wouldn't do to tell him so, he's so well satisfied with himself."

The barn-cat had been very quiet since her attempt to spring at the sparrow, but she occasionally scratched her neck with her paw to make that fascinating padlock rattle. She did it in a very unconscious manner, but she knew all the time that the house-cat was watching her out of the corner of *her* eye, and was secretly jealous of the beautiful collar.

"That's a very pretty collar you have on," said the canary.

"A present from Posy," answered the barn-cat.

"Very becoming to your complexion. 'Neat, but not gaudy,' as the monkey said when they painted his tail sky-blue," said the sparrow gallantly.

"Humph! red and yellow go well together," sneered the house-cat. "It brings out her *charming* coloring!" and she gave a taunting laugh.

"Our friend always looks well to me," said Mrs. Polly politely.

"Well, I guess you're going to be sick," said the canary, laughing. "To think of your paying anybody a compliment!"

Mrs. Polly was about as much astonished as the others at such an unusual occurrence, and gave a short laugh.

"To resume business," she said. "Now, the first thing to do is for the sparrow to fly back to the place where Nancy lives and find out what's going on, and when the best time will be for us to carry out our project. I should say 'twould be well to take some time when she's out selling her matches."

"O. K.," answered the sparrow. "I'll tear myself away for a while if you think you can spare me long enough, my dear," he said to the barn-cat.

"Get along with you!" said the barn-cat testily.

"Don't be harsh to a fellow," answered the sparrow. "You know, my dear creature, that you'll count the hours till I come back!"

"Count the fiddlesticks!" ejaculated the barn-cat, trying to look stern, but very much inclined to smile at the fellow's impudence.

"Give me a piece of your lump of sugar to take to the old lady," he said to the canary; "that will make it all right with her;" and he helped himself to the lump that was wedged in between the bars of the canary's cage. "Now I'm off. Ta, ta, my love!" he said to the barn-cat as he blew a kiss to her and was off like a shot.

Sparrow, the Tramp.

CHAPTER VII.

THE sparrow flew away, holding the lump of sugar tightly in his claw.

"It's a long time since I was at home," he said to himself as he flew along; "I don't dare to think how long it is. The old lady'll be pretty hard to bring 'round, I suspect, but she's a good little thing and will make up before long. Let me see—the youngsters must be 'most ready to fly by this time. 'Tis a shame, I declare, to neglect my family so. Well, I guess I'll take Mrs. Polly's advice and settle down."

He passed over a clear spring in the woods, and lit on the edge to drink. As he stooped over to reach the fresh water he caught sight of himself reflected in the smooth surface.

"Whew! I do look rather rowdy," he said. "I think I'll take a dip,— there's nothing that takes with the female sex like a little attention to your personal appearance, and I flatter myself I'm not a bad-looking fellow when I'm spruced up. So here goes!" and carefully placing the lump of sugar on a stone, he ducked his head into the fresh, clear water, and brought it out dripping.

Then he stepped in and splashed the water about with his wings, and ducked his head till his feathers were heavy with water. He flew into a bush and began pluming them carefully, and he certainly was *not* a bad-looking fellow when he had finished his toilet.

When he had smoothed out all his feathers he flew down to the edge of the spring and looked in, and, judging from the little complacent nod he gave and the dapper air with which he hopped to the stone where the lump of sugar lay, he was evidently satisfied with the picture he saw reflected.

"Now for home!" he said; and mounting into the air he circled a few times over the spring, and then flew straight to his home, still holding the lump of sugar securely in his little claw.

A small unpainted house stood back from the road. The whole place had a dilapidated look,—the gate was off the hinges; most of the blinds were gone, and those that were left were broken or hanging by one hinge; the shingles were off the roof in many places; and panes of glass were gone from many of the windows, the holes being filled up with bundles of rags.

A shed that looked as if it were ready to tumble down at any moment was built on to the back of the house; and a large elm, the only pretty thing about the place, spread its drooping branches over the moss-grown roof.

To this tree the sparrow made his way, and lighted on a branch before a little bird-house which looked as much out of repair as the house itself; for it seemed ready to fall apart at any moment, and the bits of seaweed and straw and wool of which the nest was made, were hanging out of the door in a most untidy manner. In fact, the whole structure had an insecure appearance, as if a high wind might topple it over at any moment.

A little bright-eyed sparrow stood in the doorway, and three small sparrows from the nest inside opened their mouths wide and clamored expectantly for something to eat as the sparrow lighted beside them.

"How do you do, my darling?" said the sparrow gayly, as he approached his little bright-eyed wife for a kiss.

But instead of answering she turned her back towards him, and looked straight before her with what she intended to be a very severe expression; but the truth was, her natural expression was so good-natured and pleasing that she didn't succeed so well as she thought she did.

"Hasn't it one little kiss for its husband that's been away so long?" asked the sparrow, trying to get a view of the face she turned away from him.

"No, it hasn't," answered the little wife shortly, without looking at him.

"If you knew how I've longed to see you all this time!" said the sparrow, with a sigh.

"Then why didn't you come and see me?" said the bright-eyed sparrow, with what she considered a very sarcastic laugh, but which didn't frighten her husband one bit. "I didn't run away. I've been here all this time, working hard to feed these three children. It's mean of you to treat me so!"

"So 'tis, so 'tis, my dear," answered her husband soothingly.

"Then why in the world's name didn't you come?"

"Business, my dear, business," answered the sparrow with a very important air; "business before pleasure, you know."

"A likely story! As if you ever did a day's work in your life! All my friends told me how 'twould be if I married you!"

"Then what made you do it, my love?" said the sparrow in a very sweet voice, dropping a kiss on the back of the little head that was turned away so persistently.

"Because I was a fool, I suppose," answered the bright-eyed sparrow; "I don't know any other reason. There was that other one that wanted me to have him,—well off and a hard-working fellow. I don't know why in the world I didn't take him, instead of a vain, lazy, flirting fellow like you!"

"I know, my dear, why you didn't."

"Why, I should like to know, sir?" she said, turning her bright eyes towards him for an instant and then looking away again.

"Because, my darling, you knew that, in spite of his good qualities that you respected you loved a good-for-nothing, lazy fellow, good-looking enough," said the sparrow with a conceited little air, "but whose only virtue was that he cared more for one look from your bright eyes than for all the rest of the world put together;" and he lit beside her, and stretching out his neck gave her an affectionate kiss.

"Don't!" said his little wife with a pout; "you don't mean it, you know you don't."

"Don't I, though?" answered her husband. "Come, my dear, it isn't becoming to you to be cross. Be the pretty, happy little thing you are, and tell your mean old husband that you're glad to see him home again."

The bright-eyed sparrow didn't *say* she was glad, but she didn't turn from him as he sat close to her in the doorway of the little house, and it was evident she rather liked it, or she would have moved away.

"You haven't seen the children since they got their new feathers," she said. "You don't know what a hard time I've had finding food for them all this time, and they are *such* big eaters! And the house leaks, and sometimes it rocks so I expect every minute it will fall down. It was very unkind of you to leave me so long!" and the bright eyes were full of tears.

"I won't again, my dear, 'pon my honor!" said the sparrow. "'Twas too bad. Come, let's make up, and I'll show you what I've brought you."

He was so good-natured, and looked so handsome and fresh in consequence of his bath, that his poor little wife couldn't resist him any longer, and their little bills met in a kiss of peace.

"What do you think of that?" said the sparrow, holding out the lump of sugar to her.

"What is it?"

"Taste and see," he answered, holding it up to her mouth.

"Oh, how delicious!" she exclaimed, biting off a few grains.

"You see your husband does think of you when he's away on business," said the sparrow tenderly.

"Let us have a bite!" called out the baby sparrows vociferously.

So the mother bird bit off a piece for each one, and then promised them they should have the rest the next day.

"They don't know their own father, the poor dears!" said the little mother.

"It's a shame," answered the sparrow. "Hallo, young ones!" he said, whistling for their entertainment, "when you're able to fly, your dad'll take you out for an airing occasionally."

"Where did you get that nice white stuff?" asked the little bright-eyed sparrow.

Then the sparrow told all about Posy and Tom, and the parrot and the canary, and the house-cat and the barn-cat, and the good luck of the little gray kitten, and how they were trying to bring about a change of luck for little Nancy, and how the ugly rats were plotting to prevent it; and the little bright-eyed sparrow nestled affectionately against him, and listened to every word that he uttered with the greatest interest.

"How is Nancy getting on?" asked the sparrow as he ended his story.

"Poor child! I pity her with all my heart," said the bright-eyed sparrow. "She never gets anything to eat but she comes out and sprinkles some of the crumbs under the tree for us, and then she throws some around the door-step of the old shed for the mice."

"I must have a look at her," said the sparrow. "Where is she now? do you know?"

"She came home about five minutes before you did," said the little bright-eyed sparrow; "and I'm afraid she hasn't sold any matches to-day, she looked so sad."

Just then the shed-door opened, and a little girl appeared, and seating herself under the elm-tree began to sob as if her heart would break.

"Is Posy as big as she is?" whispered the little bright-eyed sparrow, "and does she look anything like her?"

"No, indeed," answered her husband; "Posy is a very little girl, and has beautiful yellow hair and red cheeks, and always dances about because she is so happy. We *must* do something for this poor child!"

The child sat with her face buried in her hands, sobbing; and the sparrow noticed that her bare feet were cut in many places from walking over the sharp stones. They were red and swollen too. He flew down and perched on a bush in front of her, for the good-hearted fellow longed to comfort her.

"Dear me!" said the little girl, "how my feet do ache!" and she took one of them in her hands, and rocked herself backward and forward with the pain.

The sparrow gave a cheerful twitter, and the child looked up.

"Why, I do believe it's Billy come back!" she cried, almost smiling through her tears. "Why, you're a naughty bird to leave your wife and babies so long!"

Billy twittered and chirped, and tried hard to tell her how glad he was to see her.

"I've had a hard time, Billy, since you went away," she said, "and it's a comfort to have you back again, for it always seemed to me as if you understood what I told you, and I've nobody in the whole world to love me, Billy;" and the tears streamed down her cheeks. "She's awful cross to me, Billy, and often beats me; and when I can't sell my matches she makes me go without anything to eat. A kind lady gave me a piece of bread to-day, and I saved some of the crumbs for your little wife to give her babies, and I'll give some to you, too, because you're the only friend I have besides your wife, now that the little gray kitten has gone;" and the little girl put a few crumbs on the ground in front of the sparrow.

"If I were to eat one of those crumbs I believe it would choke me," he called up to his little wife, who was watching them as she softly sang her babies to sleep.

"My feet are very sore, Billy," went on the child; "for, you see, I have to go very far to sell my matches, and I think I should feel stronger if I had more to eat. I sometimes think that I can't stand it any longer;" and the poor child began to sob again.

The sparrow felt very sorry for her, and told her what her friends the animals were going to do for her, and how happy she would be when she found herself in a new home. "If they felt so sorry for the little gray kitten, think how they'll pity you, you poor ill-used child!" he said. "And Posy and Tom will play with you, and you'll have shoes and stockings to wear, and plenty to eat, and a nice place to sleep in; so don't cry, little Nancy, for very good times are coming!"

This is what the sparrow said, but the child did not understand the words.

"I believe you're trying to comfort me, you dear thing," she said, "when you sing so cheerfully; and it makes me forget how hungry I am, and my feet don't hurt me so much."

"The sun has gone down and it's time to go to bed," called out the little bright-eyed sparrow after the child and the sparrow had talked together in this manner for some time. "I always like to have the house quiet by sundown."

"Why, it's only just the edge of the evening," answered the sparrow; "I guess I'll call 'round on some of my old friends. I'll be back in a few minutes."

"I know your tricks," said his little wife; "you'll come home by daybreak, and then you'll want to sleep till noon. 'The early bird catches the worm,' my mother used to say; and true enough it is. It's too bad to have you go off so soon, when I was so glad to have you back again! I've lots of things to tell you;" and the bright-eyed sparrow's eyes filled with tears of disappointment.

"Well, don't cry, and I'll stay at home," said the sparrow, as he flew up to the nest; and nestling close together they talked until their voices grew sleepy, and then each little head was tucked under a wing, and both were fast asleep.

Then the child arose, and limping went slowly into the house.

"Seating herself under the tree, began to sob as if her heart would break."—*Page 96.*

CHAPTER VIII.

WHEN the sparrow awoke the next morning he found his little mate had been up some time and had given the young sparrows their breakfast; so he made a hasty toilet, and then flew off to find something to eat.

He remembered just where the finest worms were to be found, and he ate a few and saved two of the largest and fattest for his little wife.

Nancy was coming out of the gate as he flew in, and was starting out for her day's work with her basket of matches on her arm.

"Good-by, dear Billy," she said, as he lighted on the rickety gate and looked at her. "Don't run away again, I miss you so dreadfully."

The sparrow laid the worms carefully on the top bar of the gate, but kept one eye on them for fear they would crawl away.

"You'll see me back in a day or two," he said with a cheerful nod of the head, "and it's a pity you don't know that your hard days are 'most over. Keep up courage, little Nancy, and you'll soon be as happy as a queen."

"That was a very cheerful little song," she said. "I see you're taking those great fat worms home to your wife. I suppose she'll like them as well as we do sausages, though."

"Nancy," called a sharp voice from the window, "what are you loitering there for? Go along, you lazy thing!" and at the words Nancy hurried away, and the sparrow caught up his worms and flew home as fast as his wings could carry him.

How pleased the little bright-eyed sparrow was with the worms, and how lovingly she watched her little mate as she ate them and divided them with her little ones! It was so pleasant to have him back again after those dreary days!

"I think I'll move you all over to the place I was telling you about," said the sparrow. "There are plenty of fine building-spots there, and this old shanty is in a pretty bad condition. Everything is handy there, too, and I don't consider this a very genteel neighborhood."

"If we live here much longer, something will have to be done to the house; it really isn't safe in a high wind."

"Well, as soon as we get this business settled about Nancy, I'll pick out a good situation and build," answered the sparrow. "Now I'll be off, for there's no time to lose, as I promised Mrs. Polly I'd be back in good season."

"Do come again as soon as you can," said the bright-eyed sparrow, blowing some dust off his neck; "I shall miss you dreadfully."

"You'll see me back just as soon as I can get hold of that piece of silk,—perhaps to-morrow. It all depends upon Posy, you know. Good-by, my dear;" and he kissed his little wife very affectionately. "Good-by, young uns;" and he was off again. As he looked back he saw the little bright-eyed sparrow standing in the doorway and looking wistfully after him, and he threw her a kiss before he passed out of sight. "She's a dear little thing," he said to himself, "and I know I'm not half good enough for her, but I really won't stay away so long again. It wasn't very comfortable at home then, I must confess; the babies were little, and teasing for food most of the time, and she was so taken up with them that she didn't take much notice of me."

With these thoughts passing through his little brain the sparrow sped on till he came in sight of the house where Posy and Tom lived. He flew straight to the dining-room window, and found Mrs. Polly and the canary delighted to see him back.

"Don't begin your story till the barn-cat and the house-cat are here," said Mrs. Polly; "they'll be very anxious to hear it;" and Polly gave a shrill whistle in imitation of the noise boys make when they whistle through two of their fingers. It was repeated several times, until Mrs. Winton called from her chamber window,—

"Don't make such a frightful noise, Polly; you'll drive me crazy."

Soon the barn-cat appeared hurrying along, and the house-cat followed more slowly, for she considered a graceful and dignified carriage of the utmost importance.

"How are you, my dear creature?" said the sparrow to the barn-cat; "I knew you'd pine away while I was gone. I've thought of you every minute, too, and couldn't stay away from you any longer."

"Don't make a fool of yourself," answered the barn-cat crustily.

"Come, let's proceed to business," said Mrs. Polly, her quick eye interrupting a very loving glance that the sparrow was bestowing on the barn-cat. "What have you seen and heard about the child Nancy?"

"I've both seen and heard her," answered the sparrow. "She confides all her troubles to me, but she thinks I can't understand a word she tells me; and when I've told her how sorry I am for her and what we're going to do for her, she often says, 'What a pretty little song that was, Billy! it seems as if you wanted to comfort me.'"

"Well, how is she getting on?" asked Mrs. Polly.

"Worse than ever. She has to walk very far to sell her matches, to places where she has never been before, and her feet are lame and painful. We must get her away from there as soon as possible."

"I shouldn't be surprised if Posy would bring out her sewing soon," said the house-cat. "I heard Mrs. Winton tell her she didn't like to have her run about in the hot sun so much,—that she had better take her playthings on the piazza where it was cool; and Posy said, 'I guess I'd better make a new dress for my dolly, for her's hardly got a dress after her name.'"

A slight rustling was heard behind the bush where the sparrow was seated, and all quickly turned in that direction. Before the others knew what had happened, the barn-cat was down from the window and in the bush, and the next minute they saw her chasing a large rat across the yard towards the barn. Quickly as he ran, they saw he was old and gray about the mouth; and when he turned and gave a quick look back, they saw he had long yellow teeth with one of them broken off.

"Graywhisker!" they all exclaimed in a breath. "If she can only get him!"

Quick as the barn-cat was, old Graywhisker was quicker, and darted into a hole under the barn that was the private entrance of the rats, just as the barn-cat reached it. She had the satisfaction of clawing the tip of his tail; but it was too slippery for her to hold, and it slipped through her claws. She went back to her companions with rather a crestfallen air.

"Splendidly done, my dear creature!" said the sparrow; "you almost got him."

"I'll have him yet," said the barn-cat as she washed her rumpled fur; "to think of his listening again to our conversation!"

"He can't do any harm, fortunately," said Mrs. Polly. "All he can do is to sneak around and play the spy."

"I sometimes fear that he may do the little gray kitten some mischief," said the canary; "she is so small and helpless, and Major says he has so much spite against her."

"He wouldn't *dare* to touch her," said the barn-cat fiercely. "I wouldn't sleep a wink till I'd paid him off if he harmed her."

"Hush!" twittered the sparrow, "the children are coming."

Posy appeared, dancing along in her usual happy way, with the corners of her little white apron held up with one hand and in the other a small china doll. When she reached the piazza, she let the corners of the apron fall, and out rolled the contents,—bits of bright-colored ribbon and silk and lace.

"Now, my dear Miss Pompadour," said Posy to the china doll, "you sit right down here while your mamma makes you a beautiful ball-dress. You must be very careful of it, because it's going to be made of my very bestest piece of silk;" and Posy held before the dolly's eyes a piece of red ribbon with figures of gold thread embroidered on it.

"That's gold, Miss Pompadour," continued Posy,—"those bright yellow spots. I don't suppose you know it, for you don't know much, and what little you do know you don't know *for certain*. And I shall make a pocket in it, because you're very apt to lose your handkerchiefs. I showed a pocket in one of your dresses to Harry Mason the other day, and he said, 'Ho! that isn't a pocket! that's only a rag of a pocket!' I told Tom about it, and he said Harry Mason was a very unpolite boy!"

A little twitter in front of her made Posy look up from her work, and hopping on the gravelled walk was a little sparrow. He didn't seem to be at all afraid of her, and hopped about and twittered in a very cheerful way.

Then came the barn-cat stealing softly towards the little sparrow. She would take a few steps, and then sit down and pretend she didn't see him. He evidently didn't see her, for instead of flying away he hopped about as confidently as if there were no such thing as a cat in the world.

The barn-cat came nearer still, and crouched in the way she always did before she sprang, and Posy couldn't bear it any longer.

"Go away, you naughty kitty!" cried Posy, dropping her work; and running towards the barn-cat she caught her up in her arms.

"You mustn't catch the dear little birdies; I've told you so a great many times," said Posy, walking towards the barn with her. "You go and stay with your babies, and try to catch some of the ugly old rats. Michael says they eat up Major's oats, and he's going to buy a trap and catch 'em in it;" and Posy put the barn-cat inside the barn-door, and then went back to her work.

She didn't see a pair of small bright eyes shining in a hole around the corner of the barn, nor see the ugly face with gray whiskers they belonged to; nor did she hear him say with a vicious smile, "Catch 'em in a trap, will he? I guess he'll find out that it isn't so easy to catch an old rat as he thinks.

Look out, my dear Posy! you may hear from the ugly rats in a way you don't like."

Posy went back to her work on the piazza; but the sparrow had flown away, and Posy hunted in vain for her little piece of red ribbon with the gold figures embroidered on it.

"Where has that ribbon gone?" said Posy, anxiously pulling over the little heap of bright-colored silks. "Dear me! the very beautifulest piece I had, and I was going to make a ball-dress for Miss Pompadour out of it. How disappointed her will be!" and Posy was almost ready to cry with disappointment herself.

All this time the sparrow had the piece of red ribbon safe in his little claw, and was flying away with it to the old swallow's nest under the eaves of the piazza where he had slept of late.

"Posy appeared, dancing along."—*Page* 110.

CHAPTER IX.

THE little sparrow went to bed early that night, that he might be up by daybreak the next morning and start on his expedition to Nancy before the family were stirring.

Pleasant dreams of the happiness awaiting the forlorn child passed through his little brain, and he took his head from under his wing as the first faint streak of daylight appeared in the east.

This morning he omitted his usual cheerful twitter, there was no time for that; so he jumped up and looked around for the little piece of red ribbon with the gold figures on it. Where was it? He was certain he had placed it carefully in the nest, for it was the last thing he saw before he went to sleep.

"What in the world has become of that ribbon?" he said aloud. "I am sure I put it on this side of the nest, where it couldn't possibly blow away;" and he pecked apart the lining of the nest and peeped everywhere in vain.

"It couldn't possibly have blown away, but I'll look everywhere;" and he carefully examined the ground under the nest and the trees and bushes,—everywhere where it was possible for a ribbon to lodge.

By this time the sun was up and Hannah had come downstairs. As soon as she opened the dining-room window to air the room, the sparrow flew straight to Mrs. Polly, about as anxious-looking a bird as you would wish to see.

"Here's a pretty fix," he began; "the ribbon's gone!"

"Gone!" exclaimed Mrs. Polly, "gone where?"

"I wish I knew," answered the sparrow shortly.

"Explain yourself, please," said Mrs. Polly; "it's all Greek to me."

"Well, I went to bed last night in good season, so as to be up early this morning and start before anybody was stirring. Well, when I woke and was just going to start, no ribbon was to be found."

"Careless fellow!" said Mrs. Polly, rubbing her nose with vexation; "why couldn't you put it where it would be safe?"

"I did. I looked at it the last thing before I went to sleep."

"It probably blew away."

"It couldn't blow away; it was in the bottom of the nest, and besides I've hunted everywhere and it's not to be found."

"Then there's only one way to account for it," said Mrs. Polly, with a decided nod.

"What's that?"

"Thieves!" answered Mrs. Polly shortly.

"Whew!" whistled the sparrow; "then I suppose it's a hopeless case."

"I don't see why," said Mrs. Polly shrewdly.

"How are we going to find them out? Nobody saw 'em come in the night."

Mrs. Polly put her head on one side with a very knowing look, and cleared her throat gravely.

"We'll track them," she said. "Whoever it was must have left some signs behind them. I am tied down here and must trust to you to make investigations; but if you act according to my directions, I don't doubt but that we'll get to the bottom of the matter before long."

"All right," answered the sparrow; "just say what you want done, and I'm your man."

"The first thing to do," said Mrs. Polly, "is to examine carefully the premises. Look on the ground for footprints, and then closely examine the pillar that leads up to the nest, to see if the thieves came that way."

"Why, what other way could they come, pray?"

"They could fly, couldn't they?"

The sparrow looked rather ashamed of his slowness of comprehension and made no reply; but then he wasn't expected to be as shrewd as Mrs. Polly with her many years of experience.

"The sooner you begin the better," said Mrs. Polly; "and come back and report to me when you are through."

The sparrow flew off and lighted on the ground under the nest. A flower-bed stood there, and he made a careful examination. Not a leaf was out of place that he could see, and not a plant disturbed in any way.

Then he pushed the branches carefully aside and examined the ground.

"Aha!" said the sparrow, with a satisfied little nod; "I begin to smell a mice. Somebody's been here, that's certain; but whether these tracks were made by a bird or a chicken or—" and he brought his bright little eyes nearer the ground. Yes, he was pretty sure now. The soft earth was marked by the traces of little feet, but so close together that he couldn't make out the exact form; but just beyond were several larger ones, and he thought he knew to whose feet they belonged. "I guess I know whose foot that shoe will fit," he said to himself.

Next he looked up towards the nest. A nasturtium vine was trained against the pillar, and pieces of twine formed a trellis for it to cling to. The sparrow ran his eye carefully over it. "I thought so," he said to himself; "'twas he."

The delicate leaves of the plant were broken in several places, and hanging to the stem; and in one place the stem itself was torn away from the twine as if too heavy a strain had been brought to bear on it.

The sparrow had seen enough to satisfy himself, and flew back to Mrs. Polly.

"Well?" she asked inquiringly.

"Well," answered the sparrow, "I guess I've as good as caught the fellow."

"Tell me what you found, and I'll draw my own conclusions," said Mrs. Polly, putting her head on one side with the knowing expression she always assumed when listening to a story.

"In the first place, the flowers were not broken, not a leaf harmed. That shows that whoever it was, was small enough to walk under 'em."

"Very good," said Mrs. Polly, with an encouraging nod; "go on."

"Then I found a lot of tracks, but they were so close together that I couldn't make out what kind of animal they belonged to; but a little farther off I saw some bigger ones, and I'll be shot if they don't belong to Graywhisker. Then I found the nasturtium vine broken in several places, and it is evident the old fellow got up that way. I sleep pretty sound when my head's under my wing, and he might carry off the whole nest without waking me."

"You've done well," said Mrs. Polly, with an approving smile, "very well for an inexperienced hand. Now I'll give you *my* opinion;" and she looked so wise, and was evidently so perfectly satisfied with her own shrewdness, that the young sparrow felt greatly flattered to be praised by so distinguished a person.

"You are right in concluding that Graywhisker was there," said Mrs. Polly, "but you're wrong in thinking he climbed up the nasturtium vine."

"You don't think he did, then?" asked the sparrow.

"Not a bit of it," answered Mrs. Polly decidedly.

"Who did, then?"

"Not Graywhisker, you may depend on that; he has too old a head. He laid his plans and superintended the affair, but you wouldn't catch him trusting his precious old neck on that delicate vine. Besides, in case the thief were caught he would want to keep his own neck safe. No, indeed," continued Mrs. Polly, shaking her head sagely; "not he, indeed!"

"Who did go up the vine, then?" asked the sparrow, very much impressed by Mrs. Polly's wisdom.

"That I'm not prepared to say," answered Mrs. Polly, with a shrug of her shoulders; "perhaps he sent one of the young rats, but I rather incline to the opinion that it was a mouse; even a young rat would be too heavy, and then young rats are stupid. Yes, I'm pretty sure 'twas a mouse."

"What's to be done next?" asked the sparrow.

"You young fellows are always in too much of a hurry," said Mrs. Polly; "we must wait and see what turns up next. 'Murder will out,' you know; and if we keep our ears and eyes open, we shall get some clew to the thief."

"And meanwhile that poor child Nancy will have to go on with her hard life. She said she sometimes felt as if she couldn't bear it any longer," said the sparrow in a despondent tone.

"Make the best of it, my friend," answered Mrs. Polly. "We'll do the best we can for her. In the mean time don't talk about the matter; for if Graywhisker finds out we suspect him, he'll be on his guard and we shan't find a clew to the missing ribbon."

"Well, I suppose the only thing to do is to wait patiently," said the sparrow, with a sigh.

Before long, the barn-cat, and the house-cat, and the little gray kitten, and Major, all knew of the theft of the red ribbon with the gold figures on it, and they grieved sadly over the disappointment. They all took Mrs. Polly's advice not to talk about it, and Graywhisker's name was not mentioned among them.

"How quiet the birds are to-day!" said Tom to Posy that afternoon; "I haven't heard the canary sing once to-day."

"That's so!" said Mrs. Polly dryly.

The children burst out laughing.

"Do you feel sick to-day, Mrs. Polly?" asked Posy.

Mrs. Polly gave a loud sneeze for answer.

"I guess you've got cold, ma'am," said Posy.

Just then Michael drove down the yard on his way to the depot to meet Mr. Winton; and when the carriage was opposite the dining-room window, Major called out to Mrs. Polly,—

"I've got something very important to tell you. Send the barn-cat or the sparrow to my stall when I get back. You'd better send the sparrow, he can get so near me I don't have to holla."

"What a loud neigh Major did give, Tom!" said Posy. "I guess, by the way he looked at the dining-room window, he wanted a lump of sugar."

"What a loud neigh Major did give, Tom!' said Posy."—*Page* 126.

CHAPTER X.

SERENE as Mrs. Polly's temperament was, and although she gave the sparrow such good advice, she found it very hard to keep patient herself until the sparrow appeared.

She felt certain that the important news Major had to communicate related to the lost ribbon, and she was almost bursting with curiosity to know what it was. It would not do to call the sparrow, for old Graywhisker had sharper ears than he had; so the only thing to be done was to control her impatience until the sparrow appeared. What if he didn't come back until after the barn was closed for the night?

It was a horrible thought, and it made her break out into a cold perspiration, for he was a queer fellow and his movements could never be relied on. Just as likely as not he might take it into his head to make another visit to his family, or go off with some friend and not come back again before midnight.

"There he is," whispered the canary suddenly; "I can see him swinging on the top of that laburnum-tree. I know him by the way he bobs his head, and twitches his tail."

Mrs. Polly looked in the direction indicated by the canary; and there he was, swinging on a slender branch of the laburnum-tree as unconcernedly as if he hadn't a care in the world.

"Flirting with that little wren," said Mrs. Polly indignantly. "It doesn't look well for a family man. I *did* hope he was going to settle down, but I see he's a hopeless case."

"He's good-hearted," said the canary.

"Yes, his heart's good enough," answered Mrs. Polly; "but you can't rely on him. There's no knowing what he'll take it into his head to do next."

Just then the sparrow looked in the direction of the dining-room window; and as Mrs. Polly caught his eye she beckoned to him. He returned the signal, but went on saying a few last words; and from his gallant manner and the coquettish air with which the wren listened to him, it was very evident he wouldn't have cared to have the little bright-eyed sparrow happen by just then.

"Hopeless!" said Mrs. Polly to herself, as he came flying towards her with a pleasant smile, evidently caused by his parting words with the wren;

"little does he care who stole the ribbon if he can only have a good time!" and she received him rather crustily.

"Hope I haven't kept you waiting too long," said the sparrow cheerfully; "didn't see you till just now."

"No, I observed you didn't," answered Mrs. Polly in a severe tone.

"Met my cousin the wren, and didn't like to pass without speaking to her a minute."

"Oh, indeed!" said Mrs. Polly dryly.

"Anything up?" asked the sparrow.

"Yes," answered Mrs. Polly; "Major wants you to go around to his stall after he comes home from the depot,—he has something important to say, and you can get nearer to him than the barn-cat can."

"All right," said the sparrow, "I'll be on hand."

"I hope you won't meet any more of your *cousins*," said Mrs. Polly sarcastically; "because you know it might interfere with your engagement with Major."

"Don't worry," said the sparrow, "I'll be there;" and off he flew and perched himself on one of the topmost boughs of the great elm that hung over the gate.

"Good-natured fellow," said Mrs. Polly to herself, as she watched his graceful motions, "but I don't believe he'll ever amount to anything."

The sparrow sat balancing himself on the bough of the great elm until he saw Major appear and until Michael had unharnessed him and led him into his stall. Then he flew in through the little window above the stall, and lighted on the edge of the manger close to Major's face.

"We've chosen a good time," whispered Major, "while Michael is getting my supper and spreading down my bedding for the night; the rats keep out of the way while he is around. Come a little bit nearer, if you please, so that I can whisper in your ear."

The little sparrow came as near as he could, and Major put his big mouth close to his little ear as he sat perched on the edge of the manger. How small he did look, to be sure, by the side of the great horse; but he was a bright little fellow if he was small.

"Last night," whispered Major, "I didn't sleep very well. I think I must have eaten too much supper. Some time in the night I heard voices over my head, and I can tell you I listened with all my ears. One of the voices I knew well enough,—it was old Graywhisker's; and the other was so timid and weak I was quite sure it belonged to little Mrs. Silverskin, and I soon found I was right. They often go in and out at night, because they know the barn-cat is likely to be asleep; but I suspected from their whispering that some mischief was up, and I listened.

"'I'm afraid the vine will break,' said Mrs. Silverskin; 'I don't dare venture on it.'

"'Nonsense!' answered the old fellow; 'it will hold fast enough.'

"But the little mouse protested she was afraid, and then I heard her say, 'I don't like to steal Posy's ribbon, she thinks so much of it.'

"'Very well, ma'am,' said old Graywhisker; 'you just pack up and leave these premises before to-morrow night, or you'll be sorry.'

"'Oh, don't turn me out of doors!' said the poor little creature; 'my babies are so young they'll die if you do.'

"'So much the better!' snarled the old fellow."

"The old villain!" said the sparrow.

"Well, the end of the matter was that Mrs. Silverskin promised to do as he wished, provided he would not turn her out of doors; and you may be sure the ribbon's safe in old Graywhisker's hole, where it'll stay in all probability, for I don't know anybody bold enough to venture in after it."

The sparrow was silent a moment, and was about to speak when Major interrupted him.

"Now you must go, for Michael is through, and will close up for the night before he leaves. Tell Mrs. Polly what I've told you. Perhaps she can think of some way out of this scrape; I'm sure I can't."

The sparrow flew off at once to acquaint Mrs. Polly with the news; but for the first time since his acquaintance with her Mrs. Polly did not prove equal to the emergency. She gave a deep sigh, and shook her head several times in a very despondent manner.

"Can't you think of some way to get back that ribbon?" asked the sparrow. "Posy feels so badly about it that I'm sorry I didn't take another one instead. I was a fool. Any other bright one would have done as well."

"The ribbon is in Graywhisker's hole, and there it will remain," said Mrs. Polly gloomily.

"It seems to me," said the canary, who had been listening with great interest to the story told by the sparrow, "that it might be got out."

"Pray give us the benefit of your wisdom," said Mrs. Polly in a sarcastic tone. "To be sure, I've only lived in the world about fifty times as long as you have, but I'm not too proud to learn from anybody."

"Send somebody in for it when Graywhisker is away from home," answered the canary.

"Who, pray?" asked Mrs. Polly in the same sarcastic tone; and she muttered something to herself that sounded very like "You fool!"

"Perhaps Mrs. Silverskin would be willing to go for it. She's very fond of Posy, you know, and the sparrow tells us that she objected to stealing the ribbon on that account."

"Absurd!" exclaimed Mrs. Polly in a contemptuous tone. "Why, she's afraid of her own shadow! I can assure you it would take a good deal of courage to venture into any rat's hole, let alone old Graywhisker's! Why, where do you think she'd be if he came back and found her there?"

"I suppose it would be a pretty dangerous undertaking," said the canary meekly.

"I *suppose* it would too!" sneered the parrot. "No, that's out of the question; so that settles the matter."

"I don't know about that," said the sparrow dryly.

"What do you mean?" asked Mrs. Polly sharply. "Don't speak in riddles."

"I mean what I say," answered the sparrow, boldly returning Mrs. Polly's glance. "I said I didn't know about that. I'm not so sure that nobody will dare venture into Graywhisker's hole."

"Who will, pray?" said Mrs. Polly.

"*I* will," answered the sparrow firmly. "I'll go into Graywhisker's hole and get that ribbon back if it's there."

Mrs. Polly and the canary stared at the little sparrow in astonishment too great for words.

CHAPTER XI.

"Do you know what you are saying?" said Mrs. Polly, when she had recovered from her astonishment sufficiently to speak.

"I shouldn't wonder if I did," answered the sparrow carelessly.

"Have you considered well the danger?" asked Mrs. Polly gravely.

"Oh, bother the danger!" exclaimed the sparrow impatiently. "Suppose the old villain does come home and eat me up? Well, there'll only be one sparrow less in the world."

"But you're a family man. What will become of your wife and children if you are killed?"

"My wife and children are pretty well used to taking care of themselves, and they'll be as well off without me as with me. There's a great advantage in the vagabond life I've led; and being of no use in the world you won't be missed, and that's a comfort;" and the sparrow laughed recklessly.

"Don't talk so," said Mrs. Polly; "you know you don't mean it."

"Perhaps I don't," said the sparrow carelessly.

"You've got on your blue spectacles to-day, I guess," said Mrs. Polly, "and you like to make yourself out worse than you are."

"I'm sure *we* should miss you very much," said the canary. "We have so little variety to our lives, shut up here in these cages, that it's very pleasant to have you coming and going, and bringing us news from the busy world. Why, we should never have known about little Nancy if it hadn't been for you; and you are the one who is to bring her here, and now you are about to venture into Graywhisker's hole and find the ribbon. Why, you're the bravest fellow I know! Don't say you're of no use in the world when you can do so much!"

"You're very kind," said the sparrow,—and his voice was somewhat husky, and his eyes looked a little moist,—"to say such pleasant things to a fellow. I don't think I ever had anybody say such pleasant things to me before. I declare I believe I've got a cold coming on;" and the sparrow made a great effort to clear his throat.

"If you persist in doing this reckless thing—" began Mrs. Polly.

"I *do* persist," said the sparrow decidedly.

"You must take the opportunity when Graywhisker is away from home," continued Mrs. Polly. "I don't know much about his habits myself, but Major can tell you when he is likely to be out. Then let the barn-cat watch at the entrance of the hole, and you're safe from him provided you don't come to harm in the hole."

Mrs. Polly put her head on one side with a meditative air, and the others were silent, for they knew she was considering deeply about the matter. After a few minutes' silence she spoke.

"I'll tell you what seems to me to be a good plan," she said to the sparrow. "You see the barn-cat and whisper to her to take her kittens out for an airing in front of the barn. Graywhisker will be sure to see them, and conclude that it's safe for him to leave home, for he never goes out while she is in the barn. You watch from a distance, and when he is gone you give the barn-cat a sign and let her leave her kittens with the little gray kitten while you slip into the hole and she sits at the entrance. Do you understand?"

"Yes, I understand that it wouldn't make much difference to the barn-cat whether she ate *me* or Graywhisker; on the whole, I'm inclined to think she'd give me the preference. No, I thank you, I'd rather meet Graywhisker in the hole than have the barn-cat watch the entrance while I'm in."

"Well, I don't know but that you're right," answered Mrs. Polly; "then we'll leave it this way. You wait for an opportunity when Graywhisker is away and the barn-cat too, and then you slip in and get the ribbon. Major will point out his hole to you."

"All right," answered the sparrow cheerfully. "I'll take advantage of the first opportunity;" and he flew off to the top of a tall pear-tree that commanded a view of the barn and yard. The parrot saw him sit quietly there for some time, his little head bobbing about in a very wide-awake manner, and then suddenly fly down and dart into the window above Major's stall. She knew the desired opportunity had come, and both she and the canary felt great anxiety as to the result of such a bold undertaking.

Just then Tom and Posy came out and seated themselves on the steps of the piazza to eat their lunch.

"Can't you tell me a story, Tom?" asked Posy; "I've told you ever so many nice ones."

"Well," said Tom, "let me see—"

"I'd rather hear about animals," said Posy.

"Well then, I guess I'll tell you about a hedgehog."

"Oh dear!" said Posy, with a disappointed air; "well, go on, Tom."

"Once there was a hedgehog," began Tom, "who lived in a little hole in the woods."

"What?" asked Posy quickly.

"You mustn't interrupt me, Posy," said Tom. "I said there was once a hedgehog who lived in a little hole in the woods."

"But it *couldn't*, you know," said Posy, with a perplexed expression.

"He could and he did," continued Tom decidedly; "and one day he started out for a walk—"

"Why, Tom," said Posy earnestly, "how could a hedgehog take a walk? A hedgehog is a kind of *barrel*, you know."

"You mean hogshead," said Tom; "what a little goosie you are, Posy! But no matter," he continued, as Posy's cheeks flushed at her mistake; "the hedgehog started out for a walk one morning, and before he'd gone very far he met an old fox who lived in a ledge of rocks near by. 'Good-morning, sir,' said Mr. Fox, 'this is a fine morning to be out'—"

"Tom," said Posy suddenly, "I do believe the barn-cat is going to bring her kittens out. Do look at her!"

The barn-cat sat in the doorway of the barn, and moved her tail gently backward and forward, occasionally uttering a low "meaw" in a very coaxing tone and looking behind her. Soon a little head appeared, and then another, and two tiger-kittens began to play with her tail. Then the barn-cat stepped down from the doorway into the yard, and went through the same performance again. The tiger-kittens came to the edge of the step and looked cautiously over. The barn-cat pretended not to see them, but kept her tail gently moving.

Then the tiger-kittens put first one paw over the edge of the step, and then another, and all at once they tumbled over into the yard. Then what a play they did have! They lay on their sides and kicked against their mother, and then they made believe frightened and galloped sideways up to her, with their backs arched and as fierce an expression as their mild little eyes were capable of producing.

"See the old cat make believe she doesn't see 'em, and yet she watches them out of the corner of her eye all the time," said Tom.

Then the barn-cat began to wash herself, and the kittens did the same; but they didn't do it in a very thorough manner, for their little paws didn't touch their faces half of the time.

Then the barn-cat took up one of her hind legs and washed it, and the kittens tried to do the same; but they were such little round balls they kept losing their balance, and tumbled over every time they lifted up their short hind legs.

Soon the barn-cat went into the barn, leaving her kittens at play in the yard.

"That's strange," said Tom, "to leave her kittens; she's usually so careful of them."

In a few minutes the gray kitten came out and seated herself near the tiger-kittens.

"I really believe," said Posy, "that the barn-cat sent the gray kitten out to take care of her babies while she was out hunting."

When the barn-cat entered the barn, she called the gray kitten to her and told her she would like to have her take charge of the kittens while she watched for a while at Graywhisker's hole, as she hadn't seen him leave the barn for a long time.

The gray kitten, delighted to be of service to her kind friend, hurried down to the yard, and the barn-cat took her station beside Graywhisker's hole. Meanwhile the sparrow had learned from Major where Graywhisker's hole was situated, and was already some distance in, when the barn-cat took her position outside.

"Dark as a pocket," said the sparrow to himself as he cautiously groped his way.

"Perhaps I shall see better when I'm used to the darkness," he said hopefully; and he went on slowly, putting one foot carefully before the other. Suddenly he lost his footing and fell down several inches, but he landed on his feet and was not hurt.

"All right," said the sparrow, and looked about him. A little ray of light shone in through a crevice of the wall, and he was able to see faintly. This was evidently Graywhisker's dwelling; and the long dark place he went through first, the passage-way leading to it. As his eyes became accustomed to the dim light he began to distinguish objects.

"Whew! how close!" said the sparrow, as he took a long breath.

All the old rat's treasures were evidently collected here. Crusts of bread, rinds of cheese, scraps of bacon, were lying around; and bits of rags and twine were collected in a corner, and evidently served as Graywhisker's bed.

"You'll have to make your bed over to-night, my friend," said the sparrow, rumpling the bed over and scattering the rags all over the floor. "Hallo! what's this?" he said, as he came upon a smooth round object.

"I declare, if it isn't a hen's egg! The old thief! I wonder how he managed to get it in here without breaking it! I guess I'll save him the trouble of breaking it;" and he pecked at it until he had made a hole large enough for the inside of the egg to run out. He gave a mischievous laugh as he saw the liquid oozing out, and then continued his search.

"Whew!" he said again; "it's getting rather stifling here, I must hurry up. Where in the world can that ribbon be?" and he looked carefully around in every direction. "Hooray!" he exclaimed, as he caught sight of a little piece of red silk hanging from a nail over his head. "Thought he'd got it hid away safely, didn't he?" and in a twinkling he had hopped up and caught the ribbon securely in his beak.

"Now for a little fresh air," said the sparrow; "I couldn't stand it much longer."

He looked around for the entrance to the passage-way. There were three holes just alike; which was the right one? He stood perplexed. "What a fool I was," he said to himself, "not to take more notice! This is a pretty fix! Well, here goes! I'll try each one, and one of them *must* lead out." So he hopped up to the hole nearest him and boldly entered. It was utterly dark, and he felt his way for a time in silence; but the sparrow, who lived out in the pure air, was not accustomed to the close and musty atmosphere of an old rat-hole, and he began to feel faint and a little bewildered. What if he shouldn't be able to find his way at all? But he was a brave little fellow, and he thrust the thought aside. "I *will* get out, I *won't* give up," he said resolutely. "This hole *must* lead somewhere;" and he pushed bravely on.

"Seems to me I've gone far enough to take me out; I don't understand it. My strength won't hold out to go back and try another entrance." He thought of the bright-eyed sparrow and his three little ones, and he determined to hold out, for they had never seemed so dear to him as they did now that the hope of seeing them again appeared so small. With a great effort he kept on, holding the bit of ribbon in his beak. Soon he turned a sharp corner, and with joy he beheld a ray of light in the distance. The long dark passage led into the main passage-way, and he was safe.

Just as he was about to emerge into the daylight a faint rustle met his quick ears, and with horror he beheld the barn-cat seated at the entrance.

There was nothing to be done but to wait patiently and see what would happen next. The air that came in through the entrance of the hole relieved the dreadful faintness that had so oppressed him; so he sat holding the ribbon securely in his beak, but with his brave little heart beating pretty rapidly.

All at once a sudden noise startled him, and peeping cautiously out he saw the barn-cat chasing Graywhisker across the barn-floor. Quick as a flash the sparrow was out and had flown in safety to the window-sill, when Graywhisker disappeared into a hole in the wall, and the barn-cat returned with a crestfallen air to her kittens.

CHAPTER XII.

THE sparrow flew at once to acquaint Mrs. Polly and the canary with the result of his expedition. They were both greatly relieved to see him safely back, and rejoiced at his success. Then after a short rest and a worm or two for lunch, he flew merrily off to find little Nancy, carrying the piece of red ribbon safely in his claw.

It was some time before he succeeded in finding her, with her box of matches on her arm, going about from house to house.

He lighted on a fence beside her, and flaunted the red ribbon with the gold figures on it in a very enticing manner.

"Why, Billy," exclaimed the child, "how did you get here? What a beautiful ribbon! I wish you would give it to me! It would make a lovely dress for that little china doll that hasn't got any legs and arms, that a little girl gave me one day."

Billy waited until the child was almost up to him, and then flew away, holding the red ribbon securely in his claw.

"I know you want to put it in your nest, Billy," continued the child; "but any rag would do just as well for you, and I never saw such a *beautiful* piece of ribbon in all my life."

But Billy flew on and lighted again on a stone in front of little Nancy.

The child tore off a piece of her dress, that was in such an untidy condition that the little piece of calico would not be missed, and approached the sparrow cautiously, saying,—

"I will give you this piece off my dress, Billy, to put in your nest, if you will give me that beautiful ribbon. This will do better for you, because it's bigger. Now, *do* give it to me, and I'll give you and your little mate ever so many crumbs from the next piece of bread I get."

The sparrow again waited till the child had almost reached him, and then flew away as before.

"Oh, dear me!" she exclaimed sadly; "I did want it so much!" and she turned to go back with a weary air.

Then the sparrow came towards her and dropped the ribbon on the ground. The child ran to pick it up; but just as she stooped to seize it, the sparrow caught it up in his beak and flew off with it.

"I shall follow him," said the child to herself, "till I get that ribbon. I know he'll drop it again, for he's a very careless fellow."

So the two went on, the sparrow occasionally dropping the ribbon and then seizing it again as the child was about to put her hand on it.

Meanwhile Posy and Tom were out in the yard, or rather seated on the step of the kitchen door, watching the barn-kittens playing. The gray kitten played too, but more gently than the tiger-kittens.

"I'm going to bring out the house-kittens," said Posy; "they ought to have a good time too."

The house-cat was lying in the box beside her kittens when Posy came for them.

"I'm going to let your kitties play with the barn-kitties," said Posy in explanation to the house-cat, who looked rather startled at such a sudden interruption; "they ought to be out in the fresh air instead of sleeping in this hot kitchen. You needn't meaw so, for I shan't hurt them."

What the house-cat said was this,—

"I don't want my kittens playing with those rough barn-kittens; it will spoil their manners." But Posy didn't understand her; and it wouldn't have made any difference if she had, for she was very fond of the barn-cat and approved highly of the way she brought up her family. So Posy carried out the kittens, followed closely by the house-cat.

Posy put the kittens on the ground beside the little tiger-kittens, and then went back to her seat on the door-step beside Tom to watch them play.

The little tiger-kittens stood still a minute and watched the new-comers curiously. Then they flew at each other, and clawed each other, and rolled over together. The barn-cat looked on, very proud of her children's strength; but the house-cat had a very scornful expression on her countenance, as she scowled at the little tiger-kittens.

"Come back at once!" she called to her little Maltese kittens. "I don't wish you to associate with those common barn-kittens."

"Oh, do let us stay; it's *such* fun!" they answered piteously.

"Let 'em have a little frolic; it'll do 'em good," said the barn-cat. "They'll get sick lying in that hot kitchen."

"I'm very particular about their manners," said the house-cat; "I don't want them to learn common ways."

"My kittens won't teach 'em anything to hurt their manners," answered the barn-cat; "let 'em stay and have a good time. Come, my dears," she said to the little Maltese kittens in a motherly tone, "you play just as much as you want to."

The house-cat looked anxiously around. None of her stylish acquaintances were in sight, and it *did* seem a pity to cheat her darlings out of a romp in this fresh air; so she didn't say they *shouldn't* stay, and the kittens interpreted her silence as a consent. So they grew very cheerful, and watched the tiger-kittens chase each other and claw and roll over, till at last they became bold, and one of them went up to one of the tiger-kittens and gave him a gentle tap with his paw, exactly as Posy often did to Tom when she called out "Tag!"

Then the tiger-kitten turned and chased him, and how the little Maltese kitten did run! He dodged almost as well as the tiger-kittens did, and the tiger-kitten had to try with all his might till he caught the Maltese kitten, and then they both rolled over together and kicked and clawed, just as if the Maltese kitten had played "tag" every day of his life.

"Very well indeed, my dear!" said the barn-cat, with an approving nod; "try it once more, and you needn't be afraid to put out your claws a little farther. My kittens don't mind a few scratches, I can tell you; and look here, my dear, when you run up to them, crouch a little, this way, and wriggle your body before you spring, and don't be afraid of hurting them when you knock them over. Try it again, my dear; you'll do it better next time."

The little Maltese kitten did try it again, and succeeded so well that the house-cat, although she tried not to look interested, couldn't resist a smile of pride. Then the other Maltese kitten tried it, and did it so well that the barn-cat praised her for it.

"Now, my dears," said the barn-cat, "I'm going to teach you how to catch mice."

She looked around and picked out a little green apple that would roll easily.

"Now play that was a mouse sitting still; show me how you would catch it. You begin first," she said to one of her kittens, "because you've already had a lesson in it."

So the tiger-kitten crept cautiously towards the apple, swishing her little tail the way her mother had taught her; and when she came within the proper distance she stopped and wriggled her body from side to side, and then gave a great spring and seized the apple with her little front paws; but the tiger-kitten was so excited from playing "tag," that she forgot she was playing "mouse," and batted the apple with her little paws and set it rolling, and then chased it and caught it, and lay on her back and clawed it with all her four paws.

"I'm ashamed of you," said the barn-cat severely; "now put it down and do it over again properly; and mind, no fooling this time!"

So the little tiger-kitten did it over again, and really did it very well; and then the Maltese kittens tried it, and the barn-cat was very much pleased with them. "Now," said the barn-cat, "we'll make believe 'tis a mouse running. See how well you can do that!" and she gave the apple a push with her paw, and all the four kittens set off at once after it, and rolled over one another and clawed and kicked just as they had done when they played "tag."

The barn-cat couldn't help smiling to herself, but she took care that the kittens didn't see her smile, and then she made each one do it alone, and gave them very good advice about hiding behind corners and then suddenly springing out.

The children had been watching this play with the greatest interest, and often laughed aloud, when all at once Posy exclaimed,—

"Why, there is a little girl without any shoes and stockings on, and her's got a basket on her arm. What do you suppose her wants, Tom?"

The little barefooted girl was Nancy, whom the sparrow had succeeded in enticing by means of the red ribbon with gold figures on it. She had stood watching the kittens play for some minutes before Posy saw her.

"She's got something to sell, I guess," said Tom.

Just then Hannah came to the door, and the children told her about the little girl.

"Go away!" said Hannah; "we don't want to buy anything."

The child came a step nearer and said timidly,—

"Will you please to buy some matches, ma'am?"

"No," said Hannah shortly; "we don't want any pedlers 'round here."

The child sighed and turned away.

"Hannah," said Posy, with her cheeks very red, "that's a poor little girl, and Mamma always buys things of poor little girls."

"Your mamma's got plenty of matches," said Hannah in the same cross tone. "She wants a chance to steal something; that's what she wants."

"You're a very unkind girl, Hannah," said Posy angrily. "I know Mamma will buy some matches; won't her, Tom?"

"Yes," said Tom decidedly. "She tells us to be good to poor people; and this little girl hasn't got any shoes and stockings, and her feet look awful sore."

"Mamma!" screamed Posy, running under the window of Mamma's room.

"What is it, dear?" asked Mamma, coming to the window.

"There's a awful poor little girl here, Mamma," said Posy eagerly; "and her hasn't got any shoes and stockings, and her has matches to sell. *Do* buy some, Mamma; her looks so tired, and sad;" and Posy was very near crying.

"Tell her to wait a minute," said Mamma, "and I'll come down."

So Posy and Tom ran after the little girl and brought her back just as Mamma appeared at the kitchen door.

"Come in, little girl," said Mamma kindly, "and sit down. You look tired."

The child did indeed look tired, and seated herself wearily; but the instant she touched the chair her head fell forward on her breast, and she would have fallen to the floor if Hannah had not caught her in time.

"Bring her into the dining-room where it is cool," said Mrs. Winton, "and lay her on the sofa."

So Hannah, whose heart was a good deal kinder than her tongue, picked up the forlorn child and gently placed her on the sofa in the cool dining-room.

"So Posy and Tom ran after the little girl and brought her back."—*Page* 164.

CHAPTER XIII.

TOM and Posy watched little Nancy with distressed countenances as she lay on the lounge so still and white.

"Don't be frightened," said Mrs. Winton, as she caught sight of their faces, that were almost as pale as the little match-girl's; "she has only fainted and will be well again in a few minutes."

So Mrs. Winton bathed the child's forehead with cold water, and Hannah fanned her with a palm-leaf fan.

"Tom," said Mamma, "I wish you would bring me a pitcher of cold water fresh from the pump." But there was no answer, and Mamma looked around. Both of the children were gone. Just as the little match-girl opened her eyes Tom appeared carrying a pillow, and Posy brought up the rear with a bottle of cologne in one hand and all the playthings she could carry under the other arm.

"I thought the little girl would like to have my pillow under her head," said Tom, handing it to Mamma.

"It was very thoughtful," answered Mamma.

"And Posy brought the bottle of German cologne she got on her birthday," added Tom, as Posy stood shyly behind him; "she's been keeping it for you when you have a headache, but she says she wants the little girl to have it because she didn't believe she ever had any nice German cologne before."

Posy felt paid for the little sacrifice she had made when Mamma smiled at her. Meanwhile Nancy was sitting up, looking around her with a bewildered air.

"She probably ate something that hurt her," said Hannah; "there's no telling what these kind of people eat. A good dose of thoroughwort would fetch her out of this."

"What did you have for your breakfast, my dear?" asked Mrs. Winton kindly.

"I didn't have any breakfast," answered the child.

"What did you eat for your supper last night?" asked Mrs. Winton.

"I didn't have any supper, either," said the little match-girl.

"How happened it, my child?" asked Mrs. Winton, with a serious face.

"I couldn't sell any matches, so she didn't give me anything to eat. She said I didn't earn my salt."

"Who is *she*?"

"The woman where I live," answered the child.

"Is she your relative?" asked Mrs. Winton.

[Pg 169

"I don't know," answered the child.

"Hannah," said Mrs. Winton, "bring me a bowl of bread and milk. It is as I suspected; the child is half starved."

Posy came around to Mamma's side, and leaned against her in what Hannah called "Posy's coaxing way."

"Don't send her back to that horrid woman, will you, Mamma?" she whispered.

"I will look after her, my darling, you may be sure," said Mamma.

"But you *will* let her stay, won't you, Mamma?" repeated Posy.

"I will let her stay till she feels well again, and then I will find out about her," answered Mamma soothingly. "Don't be troubled, Posy; I love my own little children too well not to try to make all other children happy."

Posy looked greatly relieved.

Tom had been silently watching the little match-girl, and listening eagerly to what Mamma said to Posy. He put his hand in his pocket and pulled out his new top and looked lovingly at it.

"She can have my new top if she wants it," he said to Mamma.

"I am glad you thought of it, my dear, but I don't think little girls care much for tops," said Mamma.

An expression of relief came over Tom's face; for the new top was very dear to him, and he had saved the money for it, cent by cent.

"Do you think she would like to have Miss Pompadour?" asked Posy.

"We will see that she has playthings," said Mamma; "but first of all she needs food, and here comes Hannah with the bread and milk."

The poor child ate greedily, the children looking on with intense satisfaction.

That afternoon Major was harnessed to the carryall; and Mr. Winton, with Tom and Posy, and little Nancy for a guide, set out for Nancy's old home. A ride was an unknown and undreamed-of treat to the neglected child, and the kindness with which she was received almost overpowered her.

Although Nancy had lived such a joyless life, her powers of observation were unusually acute; and the stories she related to Posy, who sat beside her on the back seat, were so very novel and interesting that Tom forgot to ask to drive, and listened as intently as Posy did. She told them about Billy, and the bright-eyed sparrow, and the baby sparrows, and the little blind gray kitten; and in this way the time passed so very quickly that they reached their destination before the children had heard half enough.

Mr. Winton went into the house and left the children in the carriage.

Nancy pointed out the little house where the bright-eyed sparrow lived; and there she was at the door of the house.

"She's going to teach the young birds how to fly," said Nancy; and the children watched with great interest.

First the mother bird hopped down to the branch below, and the little sparrows came to the door of the house and looked down. Their mother gave a little call, but they only stretched their necks farther out and looked timidly down, as if the distance seemed to them very great. The mother bird called again, louder and more decidedly. Then they fluttered their little wings and hopped up and down, but dared not venture out of their nest. The mother bird, evidently thinking that a little discipline was required, hopped back and gave each one a little peck, and actually drove them out of the nest. Then she showed them how to fly. She flew around in short circles, and then back again. Soon one of the little sparrows grew bold, and flew a very little way and then came back; but he seemed very proud of what he had done and tried it over again many times. Then, encouraged by his example, the other two ventured out; and they too grew quite brave, and flew better every time they tried.

By this time the door of the house opened, and Mr. Winton appeared, followed by a woman, at sight of whom little Nancy shrank back in the carriage and looked frightened.

"Don't be afraid," said Tom; "if she comes here I'll give her a good hit and send her off howling."

"No, indeed," said Posy; "we shan't let her touch you."

"If you take the child you take her for good and all. I ain't a going to take her back when you've got sick of your bargain," they heard the woman say, as she held the door open with one hand.

"I take her for good and all," answered Mr. Winton, as he turned from the door and came towards the carriage.

"Nancy," he said, when they had driven a few minutes in silence, "how should you like to stay with us?"

"Oh!" cried Posy, clapping her hands and jumping up and down with joy, "I thought it would end so, you dear, good, kind Papa!" and Posy threw her arms around Papa's neck, and hugged him till she knocked off his hat and nearly fell out of the carriage herself.

"I should like it very much indeed," said Nancy, with a gleam of happiness in her dark eyes.

So little Nancy went to her new home, and a cot-bed was put in Hannah's room for her.

"Hannah's awful cross," said Tom to Nancy.

"But her's good, Tom," said Posy.

"'Her bark's worse than her bite,' Papa says."

Meanwhile old Graywhisker was almost beside himself with rage at the overthrow of his hopes. When he escaped from the barn-cat, he disappeared down the private entrance to the barn and remained there quietly until he was sure the barn-cat was out of the way. Then he crept cautiously out and ran to his own hole.

When he emerged from the long, dark passage-way into his living-room, imagine the confusion that met his eyes! His bed torn to pieces and scattered all around, and his precious hen's egg that he had transported with so much care and difficulty, broken! He gave a quick glance up at the nail where he had hung the red ribbon with the gold figures on it. It was empty.

"Gone!" he shrieked. "Stolen! but I'll be revenged! This will be the dearest piece of mischief you ever did, my dear barn-cat! I'd give a good deal to know who was the cat's paw this time;" and his shrewd old eyes peered keenly about for some traces left by the thief. "Aha!" he said, with an ugly grin that showed the broken tooth in front; and he sat on his haunches and held up a little gray feather. "It was you, was it, my dear little cock-sparrow? The barn-cat sent you in, did she, to get the chestnuts out of the fire for her? I wonder, my dear friends, if before very long you'll wish you had left the little ribbon alone! The old rat will be one too many for you, my dear creatures, I am afraid!"

In this way Graywhisker gave vent to his rage and disappointment, and sat a long time considering how to take his revenge. Then he decided to hold a midnight meeting in his house, where there was no danger of being disturbed; and the meeting was very fully attended, and the result kept strictly private.

The next afternoon the little gray kitten was seated in front of the barn washing herself, when her attention was attracted by a little mouse that ran in front of her. The gray kitten could not see very well, and she seldom succeeded in catching anything; but this little mouse ran so very near that she couldn't help seeing it, and she quickly ran after it.

The mouse ran into the barn and up the stairs, followed very closely by the gray kitten, and then disappeared into a large hole under the mow. The gray kitten was not very large herself, and the hole was so big that she followed the little mouse in. There was a much smaller hole at the other end; and out of that the mouse ran, but it was too small for the gray kitten to follow and she turned to go back. What was her surprise and terror to find the entrance closed up with a pile of hay, and that she was a prisoner!

"I understand now," said the poor little gray kitten to herself, "why that mouse ran so near me. It was done to get me into this trap, and that Graywhisker was at the bottom of it."

"The poor child ate greedily."—*Page* 170.

CHAPTER XIV.

GREAT was the excitement among the animals when they learned that the little gray kitten was missing.

"She never in this world went off of her own accord," said the barn-cat to Mrs. Polly; "she always stayed at home and took care of my kittens while I was out hunting. Something has happened to her. We shall never see the dear little thing again, you may be sure;" and the barn-cat gave a deep sigh.

"Don't be so discouraged," said the canary hopefully; "all of our plans have gone well so far, and I know this will. It's always darkest before daylight, you know."

"What do you propose to do about it, pray?" asked the barn-cat in an irritable tone. "It's all very well to say 'Don't be discouraged,' but what is to be done? Sitting here and talking about it won't bring the gray kitten back. Come, let's have your ideas on the subject. I'm not too old to learn, if I *have* brought up half a dozen families."

"I don't pretend to know myself the best course to pursue," answered the canary good-naturedly, "and I shouldn't presume to dictate to you who have had so much more experience than I have. I only meant to say that Mrs. Polly, who has the wisest head of any of us, could probably advise us what to do."

Mrs. Polly gave a satisfied "Ahem!" for it always put her in a good humor to be looked up to.

"That's a good idea," said the barn-cat, appeased by the canary's good-nature. "Come, Mrs. Polly, I hope you will give us your views on the subject; I know you have been thinking it over."

"Well," said Mrs. Polly in an impressive manner, "I have been considering the case, and have come to the conclusion that the only way to accomplish anything is to investigate the case in a thorough manner. Call the animals together, and I will interview them, and discover, if possible, if they can throw any light on this painful affair."

"Capital!" exclaimed the barn-cat, "I will attend to it at once. If you've no objection, ma'am, I should like to bring my kittens; they are old enough to begin to learn how such matters are conducted, and I like to have them get all the information they can."

"Very sensible indeed," answered Mrs. Polly; "bring them by all means, and tell the house-cat to bring hers. Please notify the sparrow also of the meeting; and as Major can't be present you will have to take his affidavit. That is," explained Mrs. Polly, seeing a puzzled look on the barn-cat's face, "he must tell you what he knows about the matter, and you can report it to me."

"That's very easy," answered the barn-cat. "Finding the sparrow won't be quite so easy. He's never around when he's wanted."

"Yes, he is, my darling," answered a voice from the flowering currant; "he can't tear himself away from you long;" and there sat the sparrow, swinging on a slender branch, and looking as impudent and careless as ever.

"Well, you *are* here when you're wanted for once in your life," said the barn-cat. "See if you can keep still in one place till we're ready for the meeting;" and off went the barn-cat on her errand.

In a short time the house-cat appeared with her kittens nicely washed, and looking as pretty and fresh as possible, and soon after the barn-cat appeared with *her* kittens. She had had time to wash them carefully, as Major was out and she could not have the desired interview with him. Their little tiger-skins were glossy, and they looked as if it were hard work for them to walk sedately behind their mother.

The house-cat was seated with her kittens beside her, and the barn-cat took up her position at a distance and placed her kittens where she could keep an eye on them. While she was making their toilets she had given them so many instructions in regard to their behavior, that they presented a very demure appearance, although their little bright eyes danced about in such a very animated way that it seemed probable that it wouldn't be a very difficult task to make them forget their dignity.

Mrs. Polly looked as wise as half a dozen judges put together, wigs and all. She looked silently around on the little group collected about her and then gave a little cough, as was usual when she had something of importance to say.

"I suppose you all understand why this meeting was called," she began. "The little gray kitten, of whom we are all so fond, is missing, and we are trying to discover some traces of her. Now, to proceed in a systematic manner, the first point to find out is, who saw her last, and where?"

There was a moment's silence, and then one of the little house-kittens said,—

"I think old Graywhisker has eaten the gray kitten up."

"What makes you think so?" asked Mrs. Polly quickly.

"Because he's got such long, sharp teeth. My mother says he'd eat me up quicker than a wink if he caught me," answered the house-kitten.

"When did you see the gray kitten last, my dear?" asked Mrs. Polly.

"Not for a very long time," replied the little house-kitten. "My mother says she's common, and doesn't like to have us play with her."

"Then, if you've no information to give on the subject," said Mrs. Polly severely, "don't give it. You must learn to be seen and not heard."

The little house-kitten was somewhat abashed at this reproof; but her embarrassment did not last long, for her sister, the other house-kitten, who was tired of sitting still so long, moved her tail backward and forward in such a very enticing manner that she couldn't resist the temptation of springing at it and clawing it.

The house-cat was rather ashamed of her want of discipline, particularly as the barn-kittens sat all this time in a dignified manner, with their small tails straight out behind them; and more especially as the barn-cat's face wore a very self-satisfied smile, as if she were enjoying the house-cat's discomfiture.

"If you don't sit still I shall take you home at once," she said to the house-kittens when she had restored order and placed them where she could reach them in case of a second disturbance.

"Now that order is restored," said Mrs. Polly, "we will proceed to business. When did *you* see the gray kitten last?" she asked the sparrow.

"I haven't seen her for the last two days," answered the sparrow. "She isn't so attached to me as my friend the barn-cat here, and doesn't follow me up so closely."

"Don't joke at such a serious moment," said the barn-cat crossly.

"It's as easy to laugh as to cry," answered the sparrow, "and a good deal pleasanter."

"Our friend the sparrow did us such a good turn in recovering the stolen ribbon," said Mrs. Polly, "that we mustn't be too hard on his peculiarities. We all know that if his manner is sometimes frivolous, he has proved to us that he has a warm heart and is devoted to our service."

"His heart's warm enough and he is brave enough too," said the barn-cat, who had a strong sense of justice; "but I *do* wish he was a little steadier in his ways."

"We must take people as we find them," answered Mrs. Polly. "Now, Mrs. Barn-cat, when did *you* see the gray kitten last?"

"I left her yesterday afternoon to watch my kittens while I was out, and when I came back she was gone. That's all I know about it."

The little tiger-kittens had listened to every word that had been said, and had a very important air, as if they could tell something if they were asked. Mrs. Polly's keen eyes noticed this, and she said to one of them,—

"Now, my dear, I want you to tell me just what happened while your mother was away yesterday afternoon. Don't be afraid to speak out."

The kitten evidently was *not* afraid to speak out, and began in a clear voice,—

"We had a fine play, and the gray kitten couldn't catch us because we dodged so. We caught her every time."

"What's that to do with the subject, I should like to know?" asked the house-cat severely, for she remembered how her kitten had been snubbed; "and anybody could see with half an eye that my kitten is much smarter than that stupid-looking thing," she added to herself.

"Please don't confuse the witness," said Mrs. Polly to the house-cat. "Very well, my dear," she continued, turning to the little tiger-kitten; "what happened next?"

"We played till we got tired, and that's all," answered the little tiger-kitten.

"I thought so," exclaimed the house-cat triumphantly.

Mrs. Polly scowled fiercely at her, and then turned to the little tiger-kitten again.

"Well, my dear, and what happened after you became tired of playing?"

"Well," replied the little kitten, as she kept her eye on one of the house-kittens who was rolling a pebble with her soft paw, "then a little mouse ran by."

"Oh!" said Mrs. Polly; "and what then, my dear? What did you do when the little mouse ran by?"

"We wanted to catch it, but the gray kitten wouldn't let us. She said our mother told her not to let us go away."

"And what did the gray kitten do then?" asked Mrs. Polly quickly.

"She ran after the little mouse and she didn't come back again, and that's all," said the little tiger-kitten.

"Very good indeed, my dear," answered Mrs. Polly, with an approving nod of her head. "You've told a very connected story, and we've found out that the gray kitten chased a mouse and has not been seen since."

The barn-cat was intensely gratified at her kitten's sagacity, but the only expression she gave to her satisfaction was to wash the little tiger-kitten's face affectionately. Then she said, after a few moments' silence,—

"Before we break up, I should like to mention that the collar that Posy gave me has disappeared. It was quite loose for me, and I *may* have lost it when I was off hunting. I don't like to accuse anybody wrongly, but it was a very handsome affair, and I dare say created a good deal of jealousy among my acquaintances;" and she looked very hard at the house-cat.

"If you mean *me*," said the house-cat, with a toss of her head, "let me tell you that *I* haven't stolen your old collar. *I* don't need collars to make me look respectable, thank goodness!"

"Very true," answered the barn-cat; "it would take more than *collars* to make some people look respectable."

"Oh, come, come," said Mrs. Polly, "don't get personal! I have no doubt that old Graywhisker knows where that collar is, just as well as he knows where the gray kitten is."

"You don't mean it!" exclaimed the sparrow.

"Yes, I do," said Mrs. Polly decidedly. "I believe that Graywhisker sent that mouse to entice the half-blind gray kitten, and that he's got her safely hidden somewhere, for he wouldn't dare really to let her come to any harm."

"How can we find her?" asked the barn-cat.

"All of you keep your ears open and perhaps you'll pick up some news. If we find out where she is, the children can probably rescue her. They'll soon notice that she is missing and hunt for her."

The Barn Cat and her Kittens.

CHAPTER XV.

"WE'RE going to play 'circus' in the barn this afternoon," said Posy at dinner, "and we're going to have the kittens for the animals."

"Nancy plays circus first-class," said Tom; "she isn't such a scare-cat as most girls are."

"Where did she learn anything about the circus?" asked Papa. "I don't believe she ever saw anything but the tents."

"Yes," answered Posy eagerly; "her says when the circus was here once her skun the fence and peeked through a hole under the tent and her saw the horses' feet."

"Poor child!" said Papa, "the next time the circus comes she shan't 'skin' the fence, but shall go with you and see the whole performance."

"Hannah," said Posy after dinner, "have you seen anything of the barn-cat's collar? Her has lost it."

"No," answered Hannah, "I haven't seen it, and what's more I don't expect to. I guess it won't be the last thing that you'll find missing. You'd better look after your things a little sharper, for I don't trust that Nancy too fur."

"Nancy is a good little girl, Hannah. Her doesn't steal. It's very mean to say such things," said Posy angrily.

"Well, it won't do no harm to keep your things locked up," replied Hannah.

Nancy came in from the barn, where she had been to feed the kittens.

"I can't find the gray kitten anywhere," she said, looking very much distressed. "I've hunted and called, but she doesn't answer."

"Perhaps the rats have carried her off," said Posy, with a troubled air.

"I guess she's gone to hunt for mice," suggested Tom, who appeared at that moment. "She won't run off. Let's go and play 'circus' in the barn-chamber. You bring the house-kittens, Posy, and I'll get the barn-kittens."

"You needn't mew so loud," said Posy to the house-cat as she took up the kittens. "I won't hurt your babies, and I'll bring 'em back all safe. They are going to be teached to play circus."

The house-cat was not at all afraid to trust her kittens with Posy. What she said was: "I don't like this way of snatching up my kittens and carrying 'em off to play with those barn-kittens. I expect they'll get to be just as common as they are, if this isn't put a stop to."

The kittens themselves, however, had no such fears, and were delighted at the prospect of a play with the lively barn-kittens; for it was not very entertaining to lie in the box by the kitchen stove, and Hannah always drove them back if they ventured out of it when the children were not there. So when Posy dumped them on the barn-floor by the side of the tiger-kittens, they began to play in earnest.

"Let's have a tiger-hunt," said Tom, after watching the kittens at their play; "and the barn-kittens can be the tigers, and the house-kittens can be our hunting-dogs."

"Oh, splendid!" cried Posy, clapping her hands and jumping up and down.

"First, we'll make a cave," said Tom, "because tigers live in caves, you know;" and he began to dig a cave in the side of the hay-mow. Nancy entered into the work with great zest, and soon a fine cave was finished and the tigers were placed in it.

"What fun it would be if they could understand what we said to them!" said Nancy. "I used to think that Billy understood what I told him, he always seemed so sorry when I told him how hungry and tired I was."

"Mamma says that animals know more than we think they do," said Tom.

It really did seem as if the tiger-kittens knew what was expected of them; for they stayed quite still in the cave, crouching down in the dark, and the little house-kittens sat down and looked up at Tom while he explained the game, just as if they understood every word he said.

"Now," said Tom, "we'll be the hunters and we'll go out hunting for tigers, and the dogs will run about searching for game, and then we'll discover the cave and send 'em in to drive the tigers out."

"I should think really and truly tigers would eat the dogs up," said Nancy, who had a very practical mind.

Tom looked somewhat crestfallen at this view of the question, but Posy said,—

"We'll *play* these were good, kind tigers, and didn't hurt anybody, won't we?"

So it was agreed that these tigers were exceptional tigers, and the hunting-party started out in search of game.

"Dear me!" cried Posy suddenly, "I saw a great ugly rat run across there."

"It couldn't have been a rat," said Tom. "They don't dare to come out here; they're afraid of the barn-cat."

"It *was* a rat," persisted Posy; "I know it was. It had a great long tail, and it had long yellow teeth, and one of them was broken off. I do wish the barn-cat were here."

"No matter," said Nancy, who was eager to continue the tiger-hunt; "he's gone now, and I don't believe he'll come back."

So the hunting-party started once more, and the dogs kept ahead, just exactly as if they had understood what Tom said about the game; and soon they came to the cave, and went up to it and looked in.

"Hush!" said Tom, "the dogs have scented game;" and the party stood still.

"Go in and drive 'em out!" said Tom to the dogs; and in they went, and soon out came the tigers followed by the dogs. The tigers ran a short distance and then turned and faced the dogs, and the dogs pounced on them, and they rolled over and over till the children laughed so heartily they were obliged to sit down.

Soon one of the tigers jumped up and ran off, and one of the dogs chased him into a corner, and then the tiger did something very unexpected. All at once he stopped and put his head on one side as if he were listening to something, and then he gave a little mew, and both he and the hunting-dog began pulling the hay away with their claws.

"They hear a mouse, I do believe," said Tom.

"They wouldn't dig the hay away like that for a mouse," said Nancy; "they'd sit still and watch till it came out."

"What can it be?" said the children, looking at each other in surprise, for the other two kittens had joined them, and all four were evidently in a state of great excitement.

"Let's help 'em," said Nancy; and she at once began pulling the hay away in large handfuls. Soon she heard a faint "meaw!" from beneath the hay, and she kept on digging till at last out walked the little gray kitten!

"You dear thing!" cried Posy, catching her up in her arms and hugging her. "How did you get in there? Her must have some milk right straight off, Nancy."

Tom and Nancy followed Posy into the kitchen; and the barn-cat, who had just returned from a hunting expedition of her own, followed too, and jumped on the window-sill of the kitchen that she might see what went on without being driven away by the house-cat or Hannah.

The little gray kitten was soon drinking her saucer of milk contentedly, while the children stood around as happy as she herself was; but not one of them was more gratified than the barn-cat, who was so fond of her little *protégé*.

"Why, where has my necklace gone," said Posy suddenly, putting her hand up to her neck,—"my pretty amber necklace that Uncle Tom gave me?"

"You must have dropped it in the barn while we were playing," said Nancy; "I'll run back and look."

After a few minutes Nancy came back, walking slowly and with a disappointed expression on her face. "I've looked everywhere," she said, "but I can't find it."

"I didn't suppose you would find it," said Hannah dryly. "I guess you've seen the last of your necklace, Posy; it's gone to find the cat's collar, I guess. Come," she continued, turning to Nancy, "you just understand that this won't do here."

"I don't know what you mean," stammered poor Nancy, looking pale and frightened.

"Yes, you do understand well enough," said Hannah. "You just hand over that necklace and that cat's collar, or there'll be trouble, I can tell you."

"I don't know where they are," said Nancy, trembling. "I haven't touched them. The necklace was on Posy's neck when we were playing in the barn."

"Yes, I know that," answered Hannah; "and you may as well own up first as last. Come, hand it over;" and she laid her hand on Nancy's shoulder and gave her a shake.

"Indeed I don't know where it is," cried Nancy, bursting into tears; "*do* believe me!"

"She *didn't* steal it," said Tom stoutly; "I know she didn't! Here, you just let her alone, old Hannah!"

"Hannah," said Posy, stamping her little foot, "you're a bad, bad girl, and I don't love you one bit!" and Posy too burst into tears of excitement.

"We'll see who is the bad one before long," said Hannah calmly.

"You ought to be ashamed of yourself," said Tom fiercely, and almost ready to cry with Nancy and Posy.

"Why, what's all this?" said Mamma, coming into the kitchen. "What has happened?" and she looked in surprise from one to the other of the excited group.

"Posy's necklace has disappeared, and I said I thought Nancy took it, and I say so now," said Hannah decidedly.

CHAPTER XVI.

"NANCY *didn't* steal my necklace, I *know* her didn't," said Posy.

"Of course she didn't," said Tom; "it must have dropped off while we were playing tiger."

"Then why isn't it there?" asked Hannah triumphantly; "it couldn't have run away by itself, I suppose."

"Why do you accuse Nancy of taking it, Hannah?" asked Mrs. Winton.

"Because it isn't the first thing that has disappeared since she came here. My silver thimble is missing too. I had it yesterday when I was sitting in the porch sewing."

"But it is very wrong to accuse anybody unless you have proof of his guilt," said Mrs. Winton.

"Oh, do *please* believe me, ma'am!" said Nancy, with the tears running down her cheeks and a most distressed look in her face. "How could I be so mean as to steal from people who have been so kind to me,—and from dear little Posy too! Oh, do *please* believe me!"

"I *will* believe you, Nancy," said Mrs. Winton kindly. "Now stop crying, and remember that we will be your friends as long as you are a good little girl. Run out to play, children, and perhaps you will find the necklace."

So Nancy dried her tears and was tenderly conducted out of doors by Tom and Posy on either side; and they proved such good comforters that in a short time she was laughing heartily.

"Now, Hannah," said Mrs. Winton, when the children were gone, "I want you to give up the thought that Nancy is a thief. She is a poor, neglected child, and I should think that all your sympathies would go out towards her."

"I don't believe in her honesty," replied Hannah, unmoved. "I made up my mind she was a thief the first time I sot eyes on her."

"First impressions are not to be trusted," said Mrs. Winton. "I shall believe the child honest until I have reason to doubt her, and certainly there has been nothing to prove her guilt yet."

Hannah didn't dare say more, but she secretly resolved to watch the child closely.

The barn-cat, sitting on the window-sill, had heard the whole conversation, and so had the little gray kitten; and the barn-cat reported it faithfully to Mrs. Polly, who was greatly troubled by it. "I'll think it over and see if I can find any way to prove Nancy's innocence," she said. "'Give a dog a bad name and it will stick to him,' is a very true saying, and we must clear this poor child's reputation, or by-and-by others besides Hannah will begin to suspect her. Yes, I'll think the matter over carefully and see what can be done. The sparrow moves his family over here to-day, and I am very glad of it. I am in hopes he will turn over a new leaf and stay at home more in the future."

"Seeing is believing," said the barn-cat dryly; "I haven't much hope of him myself."

It was true that the sparrow was about to move. Mrs. Polly's sharp eyes had discovered a deserted swallow's nest just under the roof of the piazza, in a position where she could watch what went on; and she proposed that he should put it in order for his family. The plan pleased the sparrow, and he at once set to work to build. He brought bits of straw and twine and hair, in fact anything he could find, and put it inside the swallow's nest. He was a careless fellow, and didn't spend any more time than was necessary over the building; but when it was finished it was quite a nice little house,— a great improvement, certainly, on the house in the elm-tree that his family now occupied.

The next day the sparrow appeared, escorting his bright-eyed wife and her three little ones, now fine strong young birds; and they seemed much pleased with their new quarters.

"That bright-eyed Mrs. Sparrow is a nice little thing," said Mrs. Polly to herself, "much too nice to be neglected by that scamp of a husband of hers. I'll keep a sharp lookout, and set matters straight if he goes on in the old way."

The sparrow was very attentive to his family the first day, and brought the finest worms and insects he could find for them to eat, and busied himself for their comfort in many ways, and the bright-eyed sparrow looked very happy; but when twilight came on the sparrow became a little restless and nervous, as if he had something on his mind. Mrs. Polly's shrewd eyes noticed all this, and she said to herself,—

"It's just as I thought; but I *did* think he'd have sense enough to stay at home the first night. It's much worse than I thought."

"Good-night, my dear," said the sparrow, coming up to his bright-eyed wife and giving her a hasty kiss; "I'll be in as early as I can."

"You don't mean to say you're going to leave me the very first night after we've been separated so long, and in a strange place too?" said the bright-eyed sparrow indignantly.

"Only for a short time, my dear. It's an engagement I made some time ago. Very sorry, upon my honor; but I must keep my word!"

"How *can* you treat me so?" said the bright-eyed sparrow. "You ought to be ashamed of yourself. I'll go back to-morrow, and never live with you any more!"

The sparrow considered a moment. He *was* a good-natured fellow in spite of his roving propensities. He looked at the bright-eyed sparrow; she was crying, and he couldn't leave her feeling so unhappy. He went up to her and said in a very tender tone,—

"See here, my dear! don't you know that you're going to work the wrong way? I am the easiest fellow to manage you ever saw if you know how to take me."

"I wish I knew the way to take you," answered the bright-eyed sparrow; "I'd take it fast enough. *I* manage *you*, indeed!" and she gave a scornful little laugh.

"Did you ever hear that you could catch more flies with molasses than with vinegar?" said the sparrow. "Well, my dear, I am willing to be caught with molasses, but clip my pinions if you'll catch *me* with vinegar! Come, my dear," he said very gently and putting his little head close to hers, "if you want me to stay at home tell me that you care a little for me, and make me feel good, instead of telling me what a worthless fellow I am."

"Will you really and truly stay?" said the bright-eyed sparrow, smiling through her tears.

"Really and truly," answered the sparrow tenderly.

"Then I'll think you are the dearest and best husband in the whole world," answered the bright-eyed sparrow; and she reached up her little beak and gave him a hearty kiss.

"That's as it should be," said Mrs. Polly to herself, with her nod of satisfaction, "but it won't last long. He'll be trying it over again soon, and they'll not always make up so easy. I *do* wish he had firmer principles!"

Mrs. Polly was right. It *was* not very long before there was trouble again in the sparrow's household. One afternoon the bright-eyed sparrow looked very anxious. She flew backward and forward, and perched on the top of the tallest trees and looked about in every direction, and then she flew home again and peered out of her little house with a very distressed expression.

"I know what it all means," said Mrs. Polly; "that scamp of a husband of hers is off again. I must give him a talking to. He ought to set a better example to his young family."

"Good-evening, my dear," she called to the bright-eyed sparrow, who was just then looking out of her house; "hasn't your husband come home yet? He ought to be in by this time."

"Oh! he'll come soon, I dare say," answered the bright-eyed sparrow cheerfully; "he's probably been detained by business."

"Don't feel anxious, my dear," said Mrs. Polly; "nothing will happen to him."

"Oh, I'm not at all anxious," said the bright-eyed sparrow, with a great attempt at cheerfulness; but her voice was not as hopeful as her words, and it had a sad tone that quite touched Mrs. Polly.

"He's been away all day long," whispered the canary to Mrs. Polly; "I saw him go off early this morning, and if she sees him before to-morrow morning it's more than I think she will."

"I declare it is too bad, too bad!" said Mrs. Polly, shaking her head gravely.

The canary was right. Just before daybreak the next morning they heard the sparrow come home; and although the dining-room window was closed, they knew from the sounds that reached them that the sparrows had a quarrel. Mrs. Polly waited until the sparrow was awake,—for he slept late after his dissipation, and it was afternoon before he was fully awake,—and then she called to them that she had something to say to them.

Both of the birds flew down and seated themselves on the flowering-currant bush before the dining-room window, where Mrs. Polly could converse easily with them.

"Why do you accuse Nancy of taking it?"—*Page* 204.

CHAPTER XVII.

MRS. POLLY looked seriously from the sparrow, who sat pluming his ruffled feathers, to his little wife, who looked as fresh and bright-eyed as ever.

"I want to have a little talk with you," began Mrs. Polly in a serious tone, "and I take it that this is as good a time as any."

"Delighted, I'm sure," said the sparrow indifferently, as he continued his toilet.

"I've noticed," said Mrs. Polly severely, for she was not pleased with the sparrow's frivolous manner, "that you neglect your family a good deal. I've seen more than you are aware of."

"Flattered, I'm sure, by the attention," replied the sparrow, carefully picking out a particularly rough feather and drawing his beak through it.

"My friend," said Mrs. Polly in the same serious tone, "you won't deter me from doing my duty by such frivolous remarks. I have lived in the world long enough to see many generations of sparrows come and go, and I shall *not* see a young couple beginning life start out on such a mistaken course as you have chosen, without making an attempt to set them right. Pray, what were you married for, I should like to know?"

The sparrow considered a moment and then said waggishly,—

"Give it up."

"I can tell you," answered Mrs. Polly. "You saw that pretty bright-eyed sparrow, and you made her think there never was such a handsome, wonderful fellow as you were, and you married her without a thought of the future. It never occurred to you that you must take care of her and protect her. She has done her part, and has been a faithful mother to your children; but how have you done yours? Flying around here and there, flirting with this one and rollicking with that one. I know your ways. Your family would have starved long ago if it had not been for your little wife there."

"He has been a very good husband indeed," said the bright-eyed sparrow warmly. "I have nothing to complain of."

"It is very loving of you to defend your husband, my dear, but he doesn't really deserve it. I saw you, last evening, looking out for him so anxiously, and I heard him, too, come home this morning just before daybreak, and I knew you had words about it. You make up, I know, and are very affectionate until the next outbreak occurs; but you may take my word for it that every quarrel you have weakens the love you bear each other, and by-and-by there will be no makings up, and a feeling of bitterness will take the place of the love you now have for each other."

Both her listeners were silent, as Mrs. Polly paused for a moment and looked seriously at them; then she continued,—

"I have seen many young couples begin as you have begun and grow apart from each other; but I take too much interest in you, my friends, to see you go wrong without a word of warning. Think of your young family and the responsibility of setting a good example to them; their young eyes are keener than you think they are."

The sparrow had thrown aside his indifferent manner, and listened attentively to the last part of Mrs. Polly's remarks; and as she concluded, he hopped on the bough beside the bright-eyed sparrow and nestled affectionately against her.

"You are right," he said; "I am a worthless vagabond, and don't deserve such a good little wife as I've got; but with all your wisdom, Mrs. Polly, haven't you learned that you can't teach an old dog new tricks?"

"Nonsense!" said Mrs. Polly decidedly; "the idea of a bright young fellow like you talking in that style! You've got sense enough, and you're good-hearted and brave; now don't throw away all those good qualities, but use them to make of yourself a useful member of society."

"I'll be shot if I don't try," said the sparrow, with an affectionate glance at the bright-eyed sparrow; and judging from the manner in which she nestled against him, it was very evident to Mrs. Polly that there was plenty of love left.

Meanwhile Graywhisker sat in his hole, laying plans for the future.

"It's provoking," he said to himself, "that they found the gray kitten so soon. However, I caused them some trouble, and it couldn't have been very pleasant for her to be penned up over night in the hay without food; there's some comfort in that. Then I've got Posy's amber necklace all safe. She didn't think the 'great ugly rat' that frightened her so when she was playing in the barn knew enough to pick it up when it dropped off. Well, that's encouraging too; and then Hannah's thimble,—here it is, safe and sound, and here it will stay; and then, my dear Mrs. Barn-cat, here's your fine collar that you were so fond of. You were in such an excited state of mind when you lost it off that you didn't know it had gone. Here it is, and here it will remain too. I should like to see you venture in here again, my fine young cock-sparrow; you wouldn't get off quite so easily the next time, I can tell you. I shan't go out again without leaving somebody here on guard. Hallo! who's that?" he exclaimed, as his quick ears caught a faint sound. "Oh, I know your light step, Mrs. Silverskin; come in."

Mrs. Silverskin appeared in her usual timid manner. "I have heard something I thought you would be pleased to know," she said in her little weak voice. "I was hiding behind the kitchen door yesterday, where I picked up a few crumbs the children had dropped from their lunch, and I heard Hannah tell Mrs. Winton that Nancy was a thief, and had stolen Posy's amber necklace and Hannah's silver thimble and the cat's collar."

"Good!" exclaimed Graywhisker, with a disagreeable chuckle that displayed his broken front tooth very unpleasantly; "nothing could be better! and what did Mrs. Winton say?"

"She said she didn't believe it,—that she should believe her innocent until she had proof of her guilt."

"She *shall* have proof of it," said the old rat maliciously, "and before long too."

"How so?" asked Mrs. Silverskin.

"It's easy enough to bring that about," replied Graywhisker. "Don't you see that if Hannah's thimble is hidden among Nancy's things it will be sufficient proof of her guilt?"

"But who will put it there?" asked Mrs. Silverskin, who had a secret misgiving that the task would fall upon her.

"You!" said Graywhisker; "haven't I done favors enough for you?"

"I came very near being caught by the house-cat when I stole Hannah's thimble," said poor Mrs. Silverskin, "and I am afraid to go there so often."

"Very well, Madam, then you can take the consequences," replied Graywhisker fiercely.

"I suppose I must," answered the little mouse sadly; "but if anything happens to me I hope you will see that my family are provided for."

"You need have no fears for them," answered Graywhisker. "To-night, when all is still, you take the thimble and hide it among some of Nancy's things in her chamber. Hannah will find it before long, and then we'll see how long they will believe Nancy innocent."

A little later the sparrow was flying by Major, who was hitched to a post in the yard, ready to go to the depot for Mr. Winton, when he neighed to him to stop.

"Come here a minute and sit near me while I tell you something very important," he said.

The sparrow did as he was bid, and perched on top of the post, close to Major's nose.

"A little while ago, while I was taking my after-dinner nap," began Major, "I heard voices, and I can tell you my ears were wide open. I soon discovered that the speakers were Mrs. Silverskin and a friend of hers. Mrs. Silverskin said, 'I am all of a tremble, for I've just had an interview with Graywhisker, and he insists on my taking Hannah's silver thimble and putting it among Nancy's things, to make them think she stole it.'

"'Well, what is there to tremble about?' said the other mouse; 'I don't see anything alarming in that.'

"'Just think of the danger I run in passing the house-cat,' said Mrs. Silverskin; 'she very nearly caught me the other day when I stole the thimble.'

"'She isn't half so bad as the barn-cat,' said the other mouse.

"'I know she isn't quite so quick, but she's too quick to suit me.'

"'I wouldn't go, then; tell Graywhisker to go himself.'

"'Dear me! you don't know him as well as I do. I *must* go!'

"'Well, then, why need you go through the kitchen at all?'

"'How in the world can I get into the chamber without? I can't climb up the side of the house,' said Mrs. Silverskin.

"'Don't you know the way through the shed? You just go through the shed, and up the stairs that lead to the loft above, where they keep stores, and you'll find a little hole down at the right-hand corner that leads into the chamber. I helped gnaw it one night, and I know all about it. I've bitten off pieces of Hannah's tallow candle more than once.'

"'It's a great relief to know that,' said Mrs. Silverskin; 'thank you for the information.'"

"And I thank her for the information too," said the sparrow. "I can't attend to it myself," he added, with an air of importance, "because I'm a family man and don't like to be knocking around nights; but our friend the house-cat will be on hand, I've no doubt. The sooner I inform her of the matter the better;" and he flew off in search of the house-cat.

"The sparrow perched on the top of the post."—*Page* 223.

CHAPTER XVIII.

THAT night when Hannah was ready to go to bed, the house-cat was nowhere to be found. She didn't like to go to bed and lock her out, for she feared she might come home during the night and make a disturbance; and, moreover, she didn't fancy the thought of getting up after she had gone to bed, to let her in.

Hannah went to the door and called, but there was no answer; and after going about the garden, calling "Puss, puss," her patience gave out and she went back to the kitchen. "Stay out, then, if you want to; you won't catch me getting up to let you in, if you yawl all night," she said, as she shut and bolted the door.

The house-kittens might have given her some information on the subject, if she could have understood their language,—for their mother had told them, early in the evening, not to be alarmed if she were out all night, as she had very important business to attend to; but Hannah only thought they were mewing for their mother, when they tried to make her understand. So Hannah went up to bed, where Nancy was already sound asleep in her little cot-bed and happily unconscious of the deep plot laid for her by the evil-minded old rat.

"You look innocent enough," said Hannah, as her eyes fell on the sleeping child, who was smiling in her sleep at some pleasant dream; "but I don't trust you,—appearances are too suspicious."

Soon Hannah too was fast asleep, and the house silent.

Then, when everything was quiet, old Graywhisker, with Hannah's silver thimble in his mouth, came softly out of his hole and looked cautiously around to see if the barn-cat were in sight. Not a sound was to be heard, and he crept slyly along till he came to a hole in the corner of the barn farthest from the barn-cat's nest; for he didn't dare trust the private entrance any more, and had made this new exit with the help of some of the younger rats.

When he found himself out of doors he looked anxiously about. Yes, there was Mrs. Silverskin, just where she had agreed to be; and he went towards her.

"Here is the thimble, and mind you don't lose it!" he said, as he dropped it noiselessly on the ground in front of the little mouse. "Be sure you put it among Nancy's things, where Hannah will be likely to see it."

"I will do my best," said Mrs. Silverskin softly.

"You are quite sure you understand the way through the shed?" asked Graywhisker.

"Quite sure," answered the little mouse; "I don't see how I could possibly miss it."

"Well, then, all is quiet now, and the sooner you are off the better."

Mrs. Silverskin took up the thimble and started on her expedition, and the old rat returned to his hole to await her return.

When the little mouse came to the shed-door, she stopped and looked cautiously around. Not a sound was to be heard, and she crept through a little hole under the door and entered the shed. Everything was very still,—not even a mouse was stirring besides herself,—and she soon came to the stairs that led to the loft above.

A ray of moonlight fell across the stairs, and little Mrs. Silverskin stopped a minute to rest and laid the silver thimble down. It shone very prettily in the moonlight, and she looked at it longingly.

"How my children would like it for a plaything!" she said to herself; "it seems a shame they can't have it. It is too bad to make them think that poor child is a thief. She has a very good heart. I heard them say she used to save crumbs for the mice when she didn't have enough to eat herself. Posy, too,—she is such a dear child, I hate to make her so unhappy. I believe I will keep it for my babies, and make old Graywhisker think I put it in Nancy's room. But then if he should ever find out the truth it would be the end of me; and he'd be sure to find it out, for he knows everything. The barn-cat came near getting him the other day,—I'm sure I wish she had. Dear me! what was that noise?"

Little Mrs. Silverskin trembled like a leaf; but all was still again, and she concluded it was only something that fell down in the loft above. So, when she was quite sure everything was quiet again, she took up the thimble and went on very cautiously.

She reached the head of the stairs and found herself in the loft, and over there in the corner was the hole just as her friend had described it to her. "If I wasn't sure the house-cat was locked up in the kitchen, I should think she was somewhere about," said little Mrs. Silverskin to herself, "for I feel cold shivers down my spine just as I always do when she or the barn-cat is about; but I'm only nervous, I guess."

So the little mouse went on her way, and had nearly reached the hole, when suddenly from behind a barrel darted the house-cat, her large yellow eyes glaring fiercely in the moonlight.

The poor little mouse gave a squeak of terror, and dropping the silver thimble ran swiftly for her life, closely followed by the house-cat. One pause or misstep and all would have been over with Mrs. Silverskin; and thinking of her babies at home who were waiting for her, she ran as she never ran before, dreading every moment to feel the house-cat's cruel claws; but she reached the hole under the shed-door in safety, and had just time to whisk her tail in after her when the house-cat's claws were at the entrance.

How her little heart did beat when she reached the barn; and how much faster still it beat when she remembered that she had left Hannah's silver thimble behind, and must give an account of herself to old Graywhisker! Yes, there was the old rat peering out of his hole, and she couldn't pass without his seeing her. His sharp old eyes soon spied her out, and he called to her to stop.

"Well," he said, eying her sharply as she stood trembling before him, "how did you get along? Come, don't keep me waiting here all night!"

"I got along very well," said the little mouse, "until I reached the loft, and I was almost up to the hole in the corner when all at once out sprang the house-cat and I had to run for dear life. I never had such a narrow escape in my life."

"And the thimble!" exclaimed the old rat in a fierce tone; "where is the thimble?"

"I dropped it in my fright," said the little mouse in a shaking voice. "I couldn't run with it in my mouth; the house-cat would surely have caught me if I had."

"What!" squeaked the old rat. "You lost the thimble, did you?" and he sprang so suddenly at the poor little mouse that she gave a loud squeal of terror,—so loud that the barn-cat awoke from one of her light cat-naps and quickly started up. As she appeared, both Graywhisker and Mrs. Silverskin ran.

"I believe I'm more afraid of Graywhisker than I am even of the barn-cat," said the little mouse to herself, as she reached her hole above the mow in safety. "Dear me, what a fearful night this has been! To be almost caught by the house-cat, pounced on by Graywhisker, and then chased by the barn-cat! Graywhisker is certainly the worst of the three! What *will* he do to me for losing the thimble? I shan't dare to stir out of my house till the affair has blown over."

The next morning the house-kittens were busily playing.

"What has got into those kittens? They act as if they were crazy," said Hannah, when she had nearly fallen over them for the fifth time before breakfast. "Here, you run out of doors and play there," she continued, driving them out; "I don't care to break my neck just yet!" So out the kittens went, and the same performance was gone through with there.

"What can those kittens have to play with, do you suppose?" said Nancy, as the children came in from the garden to breakfast; "they are rolling something that shines;" and they ran up to examine it more closely.

"It is Hannah's silver thimble, I do believe!" exclaimed Tom, as he picked up the shining plaything.

"Oh, I'm so glad!" cried Nancy joyfully; "now she won't think I stole it."

"I shall show it to her right off this very minute," said Posy, snatching the thimble out of Tom's hand and running into the kitchen with it in a very earnest manner.

"Hannah," she said, holding up the thimble, "here is your silver thimble,—the house-kittens had it to play with, and Nancy didn't steal it, there now!"

Hannah put the thimble in her pocket without a word; but this didn't satisfy Posy, who liked to see justice done, and always felt distressed if people were not harmonious in their relations to each other.

"*Now* you know her isn't a thief, don't you, Hannah?" said Posy in her most winning tones.

"I suppose she didn't take the thimble," replied Hannah; "but the necklace and the cat's collar haven't turned up yet."

"Hannah!" cried Posy indignantly, "I think you are a very mean girl, and I shan't ever come and help you cook any more!"

"Oh, do!" said Hannah, trying to look very serious; "however shall I get along with my cooking if you don't help me?"

"No," replied Posy decidedly, "I shan't ever help you make cookies or anything else; see if I do!"

Mrs. Silverskin drops the thimble.—*Page* <u>232.</u>

CHAPTER XIX.

THE next morning Mr. and Mrs. Winton were talking earnestly together in the dining-room, and Mrs. Polly was listening with all her might, for the conversation turned on a subject that interested her greatly. At a very important stage of the conversation the door opened, and Posy entered.

Mrs. Polly was greatly annoyed at the interruption, and at once called "Posy," in a voice so like Tom's that for a moment Posy thought it really was Tom's voice; the second time Polly called, Posy detected the deception.

"I know your voice, Mrs. Polly," said Posy, "you can't fool me quite so easy;" and the large peanuts in Polly's cage looked so very inviting that she couldn't resist the temptation of fishing one out, Mrs. Polly's sharp eyes watching her fingers and trying to give them a nip, although she wouldn't have had the heart to hurt Posy in spite of her annoyance.

"What do you want, Posy?" asked Mamma, who had stopped talking as soon as the little girl appeared.

"Miss Pompadour is going to be married," said Posy, "and her wants a nice handkerchief with pretty lace on it."

Mamma agreed to let her have the handkerchief provided she would return it, and told Posy where she could find it; but Posy still lingered, much to Mrs. Polly's vexation, for the interesting conversation that Posy had interrupted would not be resumed as long as she remained in the room.

"Her wants a fan too," said Posy.

"A fan?" said Mamma. "Oh no, she doesn't need a fan."

"Yes, her does," persisted Posy, "her's to be married, you know, and her must have a fan to blush on."

"'To blush on'?" asked Mamma. "Why, what *do* you mean, Posy?"

"Why, don't you 'member 'Jenny blushed behind her fan'? Peoples always does, Tom says."

"If Tom says so it must be so," said Papa. "I think Mamma can let you have a fan for such an important occasion, Posy."

"You are a dear, kind Papa," said Posy, hugging him; "and if you'll give me a dollar I'll buy you such a *beautiful* birthday present! I may as well tell you what it is, for you'll forget all about it before the time comes."

"Don't tell me," said Papa, "I like to be surprised; but you shall have the dollar when the time comes if you'll run off now, for Mamma has something to say to me."

So off ran Posy for the handkerchief and fan, and when they were alone again Mrs. Winton continued:—

"As I was telling you, you don't know how unhappy I feel about Nancy. Hannah insists that she took Posy's necklace—"

"Rats!" called out Polly in a loud tone, "rats!"

"Be quiet, Polly," said Mrs. Winton.—"I don't think it right to suspect the child without proof; but I must say that it looks very suspicious, and then, too, when Posy missed the necklace she offered to run back to the barn and look for it; but she felt so badly when Hannah accused her, that I pitied her and didn't believe she could have taken it."

"Rats!" called Polly again.

"She doesn't look like a dishonest child," said Mr. Winton; "but the poor thing has been so neglected and abused that it wouldn't be strange if the temptation were too great for her sometimes. We must be on the lookout, for if she is really dishonest this will not be the last of her thefts."

"The children are very fond of her, and she certainly does seem devoted to them, especially Posy. I must say it makes me very uneasy to think my innocent children may be influenced by her to do something wrong."

"I don't believe it," said Mr. Winton, "I don't believe she will injure either of them; but I would watch her closely, and if you have reason to suspect her again, investigate the matter thoroughly, for the poor child has never had any care and you may perhaps be the means of saving her."

"Then Hannah says," resumed Mrs. Winton, "that she misses a good deal from the stores in the loft over the shed,—sugar and raisins and such things,—and she is sure Nancy takes them."

"Rats! rats!" screamed Mrs. Polly again, so loudly that Mr. Winton exclaimed,—

"What a nuisance that bird is when she screams so! I wonder if she does see a rat! She sticks to it so persistently I shouldn't wonder;" and he rose and looked out of the window. There were no signs of rats there, however; the only living creatures he saw were the little sparrows who had a nest under the eaves of the piazza.

"Well, I must go," he said, as he came back from the window. "Major will think that I have forgotten he is waiting harnessed;" and soon Mrs. Polly and the canary were the only occupants of the dining-room.

"Provoking!" exclaimed Mrs. Polly. "I do think human beings are the stupidest things! Here I told them, as plainly as could be, that the rats stole Posy's necklace and the sugar and raisins, and they couldn't understand! Talk about animals not being as intelligent as human beings! Why can't they understand us as well as we can them, I should like to know!"

"It does seem strange they didn't know what you meant," said the canary; "I am sure you spoke plainly enough."

"I can't understand," said Mrs. Polly in an irritable tone, "how they can be so stupid. Here they know that the rats steal Major's oats, and that it is the habit of rats to steal anything that attracts their attention, and yet it never occurs to them that they are the ones that take the sugar and raisins! If the barn-cat and the house-cat were not so jealous of each other and didn't quarrel all the time, they might catch old Graywhisker, for he is the one that makes all the trouble; but no, they can't work together, and while one is at one end of the hole, he slips out of the other. If they could only agree together for one to watch at each end, they'd catch him fast enough."

"There'll be trouble as long as he lives," sighed the canary. "Posy said Michael was going to set a trap for him."

"Much good that will do," replied Mrs. Polly scornfully; "he's too old a head to walk into a trap."

All this time the barn-cat and the house-cat had been devoting all their energies to catching Graywhisker. It was very seldom that either one or the other was not in the way when he attempted to venture out; and the barn-cat set the gray kitten and the little tiger-kittens to watch when she could not.

The gray kitten had grown stronger than she was when she first came to live there, and the young tiger-kittens considered themselves a match even for Graywhisker. As for poor little Mrs. Silverskin, she dared not venture out at all in these troubled times; for, between her fear of Graywhisker and the cats, times were hard indeed.

Old Graywhisker felt that his case was becoming desperate. He sat in his house and looked around on his once well-filled larder. Not a crust, or rind of cheese or pork, was left. His last crumb was gone, and where was he to get more? It was now several days since he had dared venture out, and it was evident the cats were bent on his destruction, for there was now never a time when one of them was not about. He knew he must make a bold move and try to escape from the cats or else die of starvation.

"You'll never catch Graywhisker there," said the barn-cat to the house-cat, who was watching the hole outside the barn. "He comes out by half a dozen different ways."

"Then why don't you catch him yourself? If you know so much better than anybody else, I should think it would be easy enough," retorted the house-cat angrily.

"I intend to catch him," replied the barn-cat; "he'll soon be starved out and *have* to leave his hole."

"And I intend to catch him too," said the house-cat.

"Between you both you'll lose him," said the sparrow to himself, who, perched on a pear-tree, had overheard the conversation.

Meanwhile Graywhisker grew more and more hungry. He searched his house over and over again, hoping that he might have overlooked a crust, but he could find nothing. Then his eyes fell on the barn-cat's collar, and he gave the ugly grin that displayed the broken front tooth so unpleasantly. "If I can't make you ornamental I can at least make you useful, my dear Mrs. Barn-cat," he said. "Leather is not as much to my taste as pork or cheese or sugar, but it is better than nothing; so here goes!" and taking the pretty red collar between his forepaws, he bit out a large piece. "Not much flavor," he continued; "but if you think of a nice bit of toasted cheese or a delicate piece of pork rind while it's going down, it isn't so bad."

Soon nothing remained of the gay little collar that had been the barn-cat's pride, but the plate on which to engrave the name and the padlock that used to tinkle so musically; but after the leather was eaten up, Graywhisker became desperate indeed!

"If I could get hold of one of those tiger-kittens, wouldn't it be a treat?" he exclaimed, with a horrible grimace. "I *will* venture out, cost what it may. I don't know as it would be any worse to be caught by the cats than to die here slowly by inches. Oh, if I could only get hold of one of those young rats or Mrs. Silverskin! I'd make them bring me something to eat,— they are so much lighter than I am they can slip along more easily."

The barn-cat sat behind a post in the barn, where she could hear and see without being seen, and the house-cat was watching a hole outside with great perseverance.

"He can't come out without one of us seeing him," said the barn-cat to herself; "I am sure of that. One thing is certain; he can't stand it much longer. He *must* venture out soon for food, and then—"

Yes, she was right; he was coming out at last,—that was his long gray nose looking out of his hole, and those his small sharp eyes. Hardly daring to breathe, the barn-cat watched every motion. He looked anxiously around in every direction, and then stole softly along. The barn-cat did not stir until he was directly opposite the post where she was concealed, and then gave a sudden spring, and her sharp claws were fastened in his back, and the old thief and plotter was a prisoner!

Posy takes a peanut from Mrs. Polly's cage.—*Page* <u>239.</u>

CHAPTER XX.

"COME to the barn, the three of yees, till ye see the big rat the barn-cat is after catching," said Michael to the children the next morning; and off they started, in such a hurry that poor little Posy tripped over a stone and scraped the skin off her chubby little hands.

"Be a brave girl and don't cry," said Tom encouragingly, looking at Posy's face, that was distorted from the effort she made to keep from crying.

"No," said Posy, swallowing very hard and winking back the tears; "I don't cry at trifles, do I, Tom? Some girls would cry, wouldn't they, Tom? The tears might come into my eyes just a little bit, you know, but I wouldn't cry;" and two great tears rolled down Posy's cheeks as she spoke.

Nancy and Tom wiped the little hands very tenderly, and Tom's praise of her fortitude made the smarting much easier to bear; and in a few minutes the three children were on their way to the barn again.

On the barn-floor lay a large rat, gray around the nose from age, and nearly as large as the barn-cat herself, who sat near by.

"He's an old fellow," said Michael; "ye can see that by the gray beard of him."

"Look at his long yellow teeth," said Tom, stooping to examine the rat more closely, "and one of them is broken off. I guess 'twas done in a fight, don't you, Michael?"

"It's as like as not," answered Michael.

"How pleased the cats seem to be!" said Posy, looking from the barn-cat, who watched the dead rat with so much satisfaction, to the gray kitten, who looked on from behind her, and the house-cat, who appeared at the door and looked in with great interest. The tiger-kittens came too, and were so curious they couldn't see all they wanted to without going up to the rat and smelling around him, till their mother gave a little "meaw" and drove them back. Then the house-kittens came too, and peeped around the corner.

"I'm glad he's out of the way, even if I didn't catch him myself," said the house-cat.

The barn-cat was of too generous a disposition to boast of her victory. "It doesn't make any difference who caught him, now that he *is* caught.

What I want to see next is, these boards ripped up and the old fellow's nest examined; for I am certain my collar and Posy's necklace will be found there."

"I wonder they don't think of it," said the house-cat; "but human beings are so stupid I declare I've no patience with them."

"The cats mew just as if they were talking it over," said Tom.

"I shouldn't wonder if they were," said Posy; "I wish we knew what they were saying."

"I wish you did," said the house-cat, "but that would be expecting too much of you."

The sparrow, too, had heard the news, and perched on the window to get a look at the notorious Graywhisker who had caused so much mischief.

"I should have been in a pretty fix if that old fellow had come home and found me in his house that time," he said to himself; "one thing is certain, I shouldn't be sitting here now if he had. Hallo, my dear! you came to get a sight of the old villain, did you?" he said to the bright-eyed sparrow who lit beside him.

"I do believe those sparrows have come to see the rat too," said Nancy.

Major, also, had turned around in his box-stall and faced the little group assembled around the dead rat, and appeared to take great interest in the event.

"Now, the only thing left to do is to tear up those boards and bring the old fellow's nest to light," neighed Major.

"I guess Major is saying he's glad the old rat won't be able to steal any more of his oats, don't you, Tom?" said Posy, going up to the gentle horse and stroking his soft nose.

"It's more likely he's after asking yees for the apples ye have in the hands of yees," answered Michael.

Major gave him as scornful a look as his mild eyes were capable of giving, and then rubbed his nose affectionately against the little hand that stroked him, in order to show his appreciation of the sympathy she had with his feelings.

"Papa," cried Tom and Posy together, as Mr. Winton came out of the house, "do come and see this awful big rat the barn-cat caught last night."

"He was an old stager, and no mistake," said Papa, looking at him. "I want you, Michael, to take up these boards and destroy all the old nests. I don't doubt there are a good many of them."

The barn-cat was so delighted that she completely forgot her dignity, and catching sight of the tiger-kittens and house-kittens at play in the yard, raced up to them and chased them around till they thought she had suddenly lost her wits.

"Well, I declare," said the house-cat, who was too well bred to forget *her* dignity in such a manner, "I thought you had a fit."

"It did me good," said the barn-cat; "I had to do something or I should have exploded with joy."

That afternoon, Michael, armed with a crowbar and hammer, went out to the barn, followed by the children, who seated themselves comfortably on the oat-box, where they could obtain a good view of Michael as he tore up the boards of the floor.

Placing the crowbar under one of the planks, he gradually pried it up and laid it on one side. The children peeped curiously in, but to their great disappointment nothing was to be seen.

"It's here where they've been," said Michael; "I see the tracks of 'em."

Then another plank was pried up and laid aside, and Michael looked down and carefully examined the ground. "It's here where the old villain lived, I'll be bound," he exclaimed.

Down jumped the children from the oat-box and stood beside Michael.

"There's his nest," cried Tom excitedly,—"that bunch of rags and twine in the corner."

"It's right ye are," replied Michael.

"What's that yellow thing there under that rag?" asked Tom.

Michael stooped and picked up the object that had attracted Tom's attention.

"My amber necklace," shrieked Posy joyfully. "Oh, I'm so glad! Now they won't say you took it any more, Nancy;" and snatching the necklace from Michael's hand, she darted out of the barn, calling "Mamma" so loudly that Mrs. Winton was at the door almost as soon as Posy was.

"My amber necklace," cried Posy, waving it frantically over her head. "It was in the old rat's nest. Come and see where he lived."

Mrs. Winton followed Posy to the barn, and looked into what had once been Graywhisker's home.

"It was right there, under that old rag," cried Tom; "I saw it first."

"What is that little thing shining there?" asked Mrs. Winton, pointing to a bright spot.

Michael picked it up and handed it to her.

"Why, it must be the padlock to the barn-cat's collar!" exclaimed Mrs. Winton. "What a thief the old fellow was! I know now where the sugar and raisins must have gone. Tell Hannah to come here a minute, Tom."

Tom was off like a shot and soon returned, bringing Hannah, who looked greatly astonished at the unusual message.

"Hannah," said Mrs. Winton, holding up the amber necklace, "Posy's necklace has been found in this old rat-hole, and also what is left of the barn-cat's collar. You see your suspicions were unfounded. The thief who has caused so much mischief is now dead, and I think you will find that your stores in the loft will not disappear as fast as they used to."

Hannah was silent, and her face flushed.

"You do believe, *now*, that Nancy isn't a thief, don't you, Hannah?" said Posy earnestly.

"Yes," said Hannah slowly, for it cost her a great effort to acknowledge she had made a mistake; "I see I was mistaken, and I am sorry. I can't say no more than that, as I know."

"Hannah," said Posy, with her sweetest smile, "I *don't* think you are a mean girl, and I *will* help you cook whenever you want me to."

"Then I'm all right," answered Hannah cheerfully.

It would be hard to tell how happy Nancy was at the favorable turn affairs had taken; and if such a thing were possible, the animals, who had been the means of bringing it to pass, were even happier than she was. Mrs. Polly was so excited that for several days she talked the family almost to death, and the canary sang till it seemed as if his little throat would burst.

The sparrow settled down into quite a model husband and father, and very seldom relapsed into his old habits. He and the little bright-eyed sparrow continued to be very fond of each other, and brought up many broods of young sparrows,—some of them lively young fellows like their father and as fond of keeping late hours as he used to be, and others as bright-eyed and domestic as the bright-eyed sparrow herself.

The barn-cat and the house-cat continued to disagree in their ideas of education, but their kittens associated together with great amiability and did not share the jealousies of their mothers.

Little Nancy never left the kind friends who had befriended her, and was so devoted to Posy and made her so happy that a new nurse never appeared, and the children became more attached to her every day, if such a thing were possible.

Milton Keynes UK
Ingram Content Group UK Ltd.
UKHW012314040624
443649UK00007B/616

9 789361 470264